Godi + Zidrou

Ducoboo

Colour work: Véronique Grobet

9th CINEBOOK
The 9th Art Publisher

Original title: L'élève Ducobu – La lutte des classes

Original edition: © Les Editions du Lombard (Dargaud-Lombard SA), 1999
by Godi & Zidrou
www.lelombard.com
All rights reserved

English translation: © 2010 Cinebook Ltd

Translator: Luke Spear
Lettering and text layout: Imadjinn sarl
Printed in Spain by Just Colour Graphic

This edition first published in Great Britain in 2010 by
Cinebook Ltd
56 Beech Avenue
Canterbury, Kent
CT4 7TA
www.cinebook.com

A CIP catalogue record for this book
is available from the British Library

ISBN 978-1-84918-031-3

9th CINEBOOK
The 9th Art Publisher

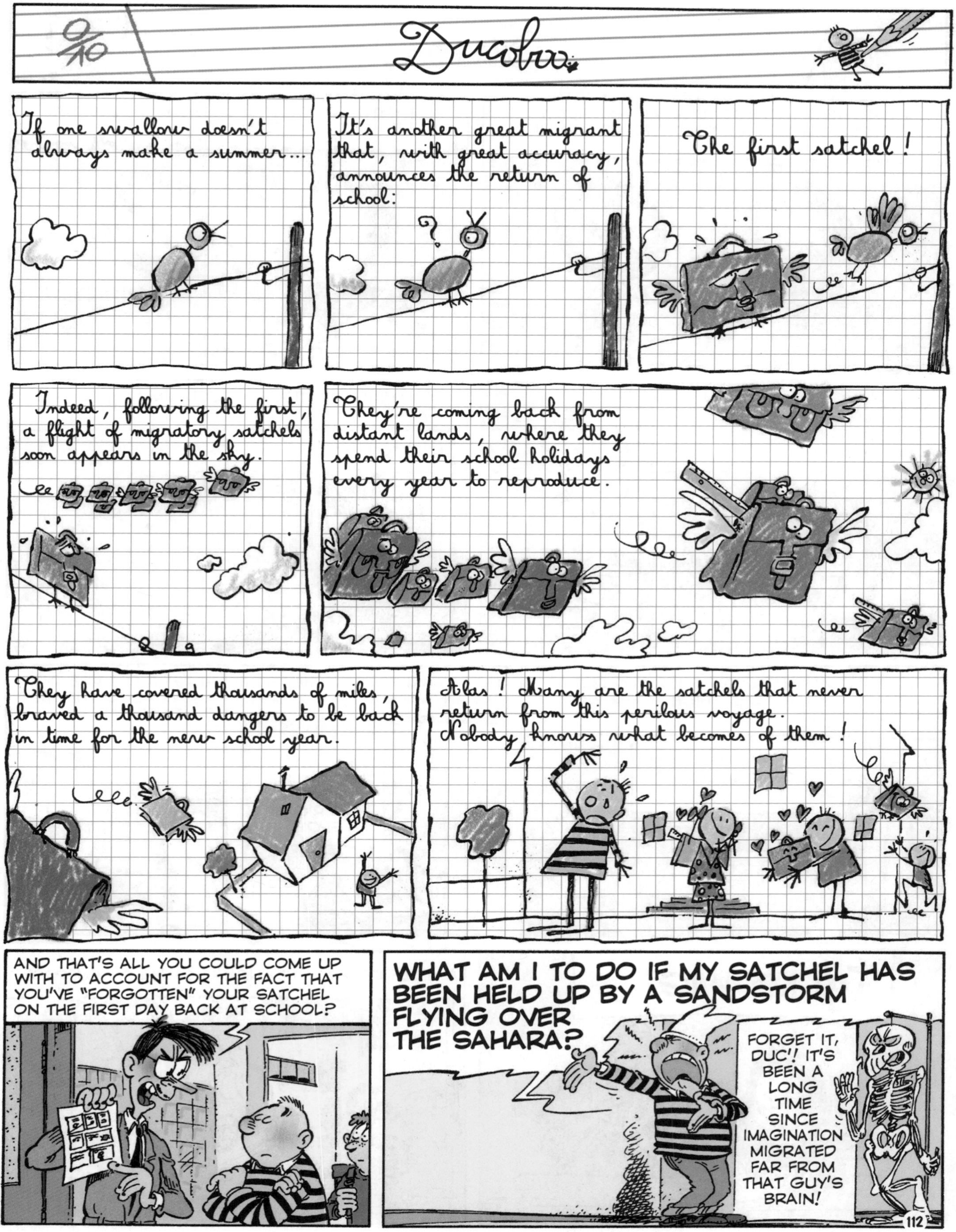
9/10
Ducobu
If one swallow doesn't always make a summer...
It's another great migrant that, with great accuracy, announces the return of school:
?
The first satchel!
Indeed, following the first, a flight of migratory satchels soon appears in the sky.
They're coming back from distant lands, where they spend their school holidays every year to reproduce.
They have covered thousands of miles, braved a thousand dangers to be back in time for the new school year.
Alas! Many are the satchels that never return from this perilous voyage. Nobody knows what becomes of them!
AND THAT'S ALL YOU COULD COME UP WITH TO ACCOUNT FOR THE FACT THAT YOU'VE "FORGOTTEN" YOUR SATCHEL ON THE FIRST DAY BACK AT SCHOOL?
WHAT AM I TO DO IF MY SATCHEL HAS BEEN HELD UP BY A SANDSTORM FLYING OVER THE SAHARA?
FORGET IT, DUC! IT'S BEEN A LONG TIME SINCE IMAGINATION MIGRATED FAR FROM THAT GUY'S BRAIN!
112

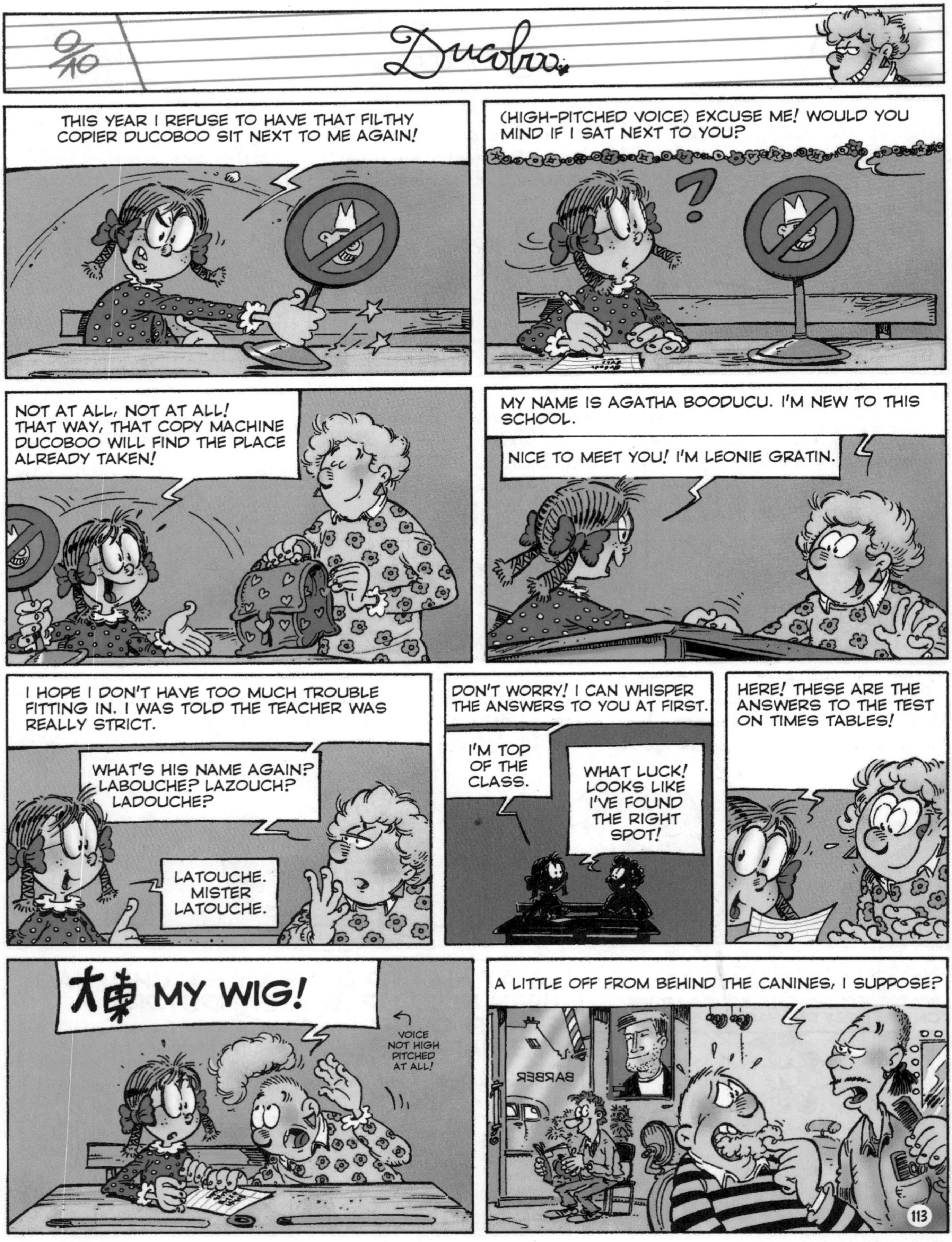
9/10
Ducoboo
THIS YEAR I REFUSE TO HAVE THAT FILTHY COPIER DUCOBOO SIT NEXT TO ME AGAIN!
(HIGH-PITCHED VOICE) EXCUSE ME! WOULD YOU MIND IF I SAT NEXT TO YOU?
?
NOT AT ALL, NOT AT ALL! THAT WAY, THAT COPY MACHINE DUCOBOO WILL FIND THE PLACE ALREADY TAKEN!
MY NAME IS AGATHA BOODUCU. I'M NEW TO THIS SCHOOL.
NICE TO MEET YOU! I'M LEONIE GRATIN.
I HOPE I DON'T HAVE TOO MUCH TROUBLE FITTING IN. I WAS TOLD THE TEACHER WAS REALLY STRICT.
WHAT'S HIS NAME AGAIN? LABOUCHE? LAZOUCH? LADOUCHE?
LATOUCHE. MISTER LATOUCHE.
DON'T WORRY! I CAN WHISPER THE ANSWERS TO YOU AT FIRST.
I'M TOP OF THE CLASS.
WHAT LUCK! LOOKS LIKE I'VE FOUND THE RIGHT SPOT!
HERE! THESE ARE THE ANSWERS TO THE TEST ON TIMES TABLES!
MY WIG!
VOICE NOT HIGH PITCHED AT ALL!
A LITTLE OFF FROM BEHIND THE CANINES, I SUPPOSE?
BARBER
113

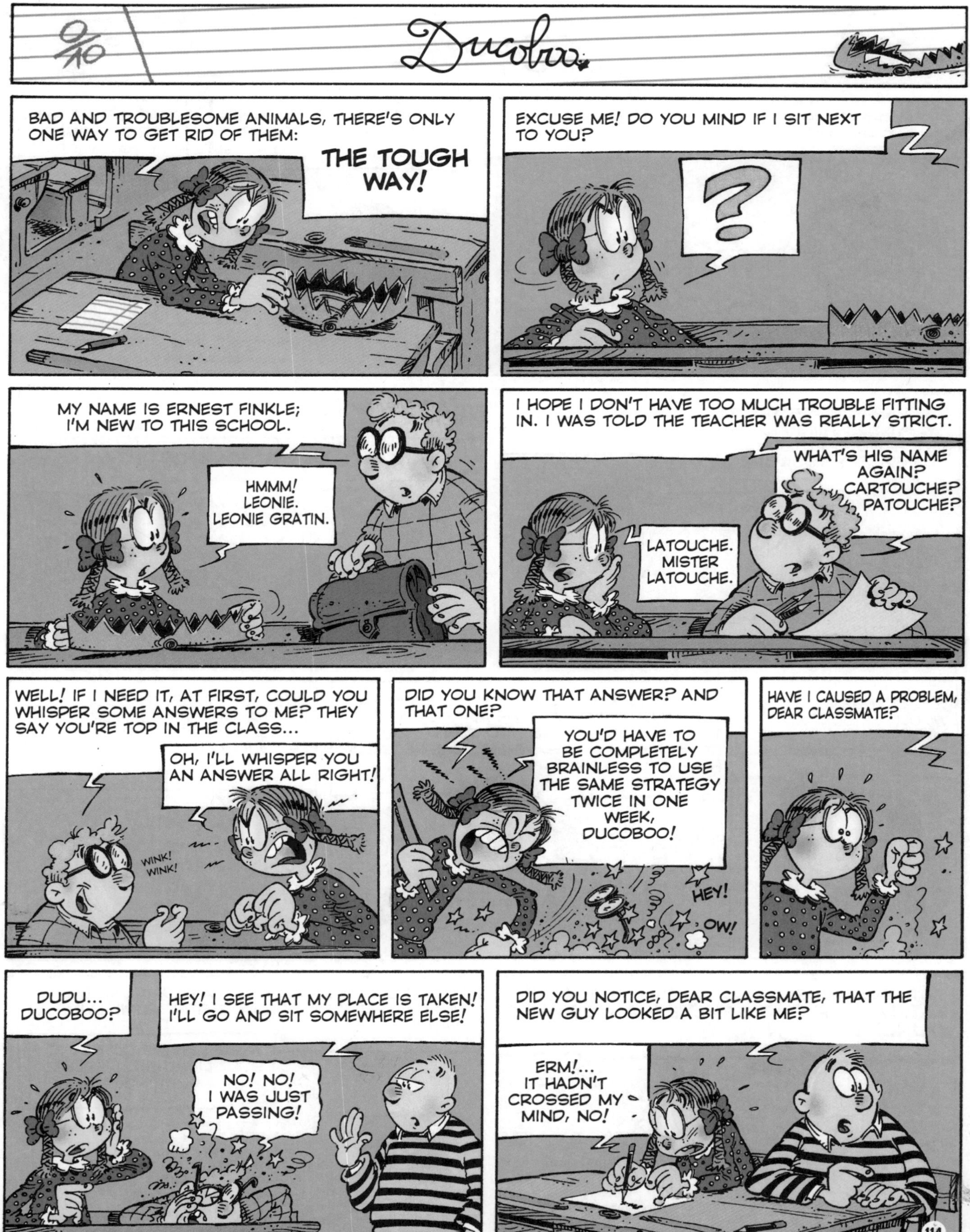
Ducoboo
BAD AND TROUBLESOME ANIMALS, THERE'S ONLY ONE WAY TO GET RID OF THEM:
THE TOUGH WAY!
EXCUSE ME! DO YOU MIND IF I SIT NEXT TO YOU?
?
MY NAME IS ERNEST FINKLE; I'M NEW TO THIS SCHOOL.
HMMM! LEONIE. LEONIE GRATIN.
I HOPE I DON'T HAVE TOO MUCH TROUBLE FITTING IN. I WAS TOLD THE TEACHER WAS REALLY STRICT.
WHAT'S HIS NAME AGAIN? CARTOUCHE? PATOUCHE?
LATOUCHE. MISTER LATOUCHE.
WELL! IF I NEED IT, AT FIRST, COULD YOU WHISPER SOME ANSWERS TO ME? THEY SAY YOU'RE TOP IN THE CLASS...
OH, I'LL WHISPER YOU AN ANSWER ALL RIGHT!
WINK! WINK!
DID YOU KNOW THAT ANSWER? AND THAT ONE?
YOU'D HAVE TO BE COMPLETELY BRAINLESS TO USE THE SAME STRATEGY TWICE IN ONE WEEK, DUCOBOO!
HEY!
OW!
HAVE I CAUSED A PROBLEM, DEAR CLASSMATE?
DUDU... DUCOBOO?
HEY! I SEE THAT MY PLACE IS TAKEN! I'LL GO AND SIT SOMEWHERE ELSE!
NO! NO! I WAS JUST PASSING!
DID YOU NOTICE, DEAR CLASSMATE, THAT THE NEW GUY LOOKED A BIT LIKE ME?
ERM!... IT HADN'T CROSSED MY MIND, NO!
114

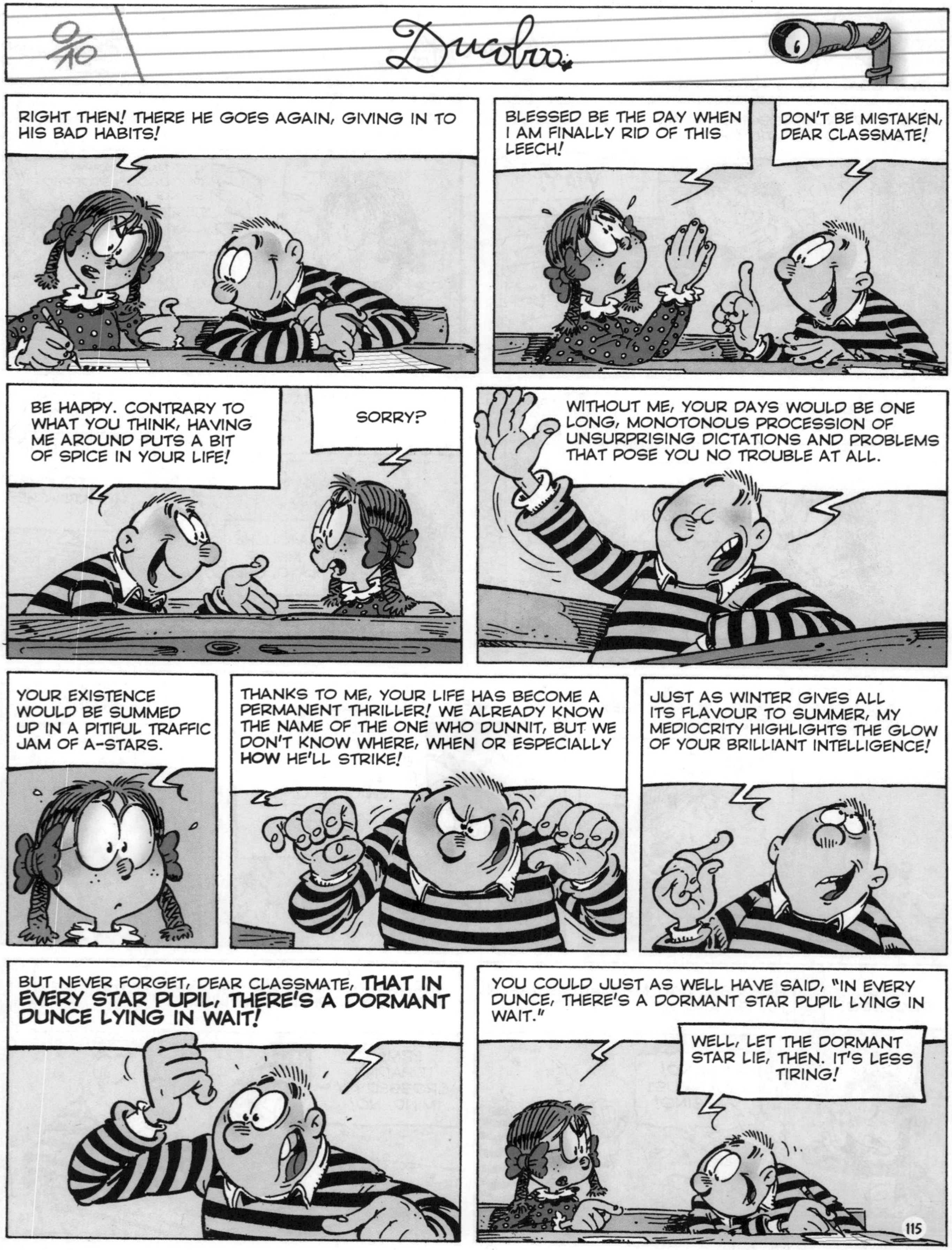
0/10
Ducobu
RIGHT THEN! THERE HE GOES AGAIN, GIVING IN TO HIS BAD HABITS!
BLESSED BE THE DAY WHEN I AM FINALLY RID OF THIS LEECH!
DON'T BE MISTAKEN, DEAR CLASSMATE!
BE HAPPY. CONTRARY TO WHAT YOU THINK, HAVING ME AROUND PUTS A BIT OF SPICE IN YOUR LIFE!
SORRY?
WITHOUT ME, YOUR DAYS WOULD BE ONE LONG, MONOTONOUS PROCESSION OF UNSURPRISING DICTATIONS AND PROBLEMS THAT POSE YOU NO TROUBLE AT ALL.
YOUR EXISTENCE WOULD BE SUMMED UP IN A PITIFUL TRAFFIC JAM OF A-STARS.
THANKS TO ME, YOUR LIFE HAS BECOME A PERMANENT THRILLER! WE ALREADY KNOW THE NAME OF THE ONE WHO DUNNIT, BUT WE DON'T KNOW WHERE, WHEN OR ESPECIALLY **HOW** HE'LL STRIKE!
JUST AS WINTER GIVES ALL ITS FLAVOUR TO SUMMER, MY MEDIOCRITY HIGHLIGHTS THE GLOW OF YOUR BRILLIANT INTELLIGENCE!
BUT NEVER FORGET, DEAR CLASSMATE, **THAT IN EVERY STAR PUPIL, THERE'S A DORMANT DUNCE LYING IN WAIT!**
YOU COULD JUST AS WELL HAVE SAID, "IN EVERY DUNCE, THERE'S A DORMANT STAR PUPIL LYING IN WAIT."
WELL, LET THE DORMANT STAR LIE, THEN. IT'S LESS TIRING!
115

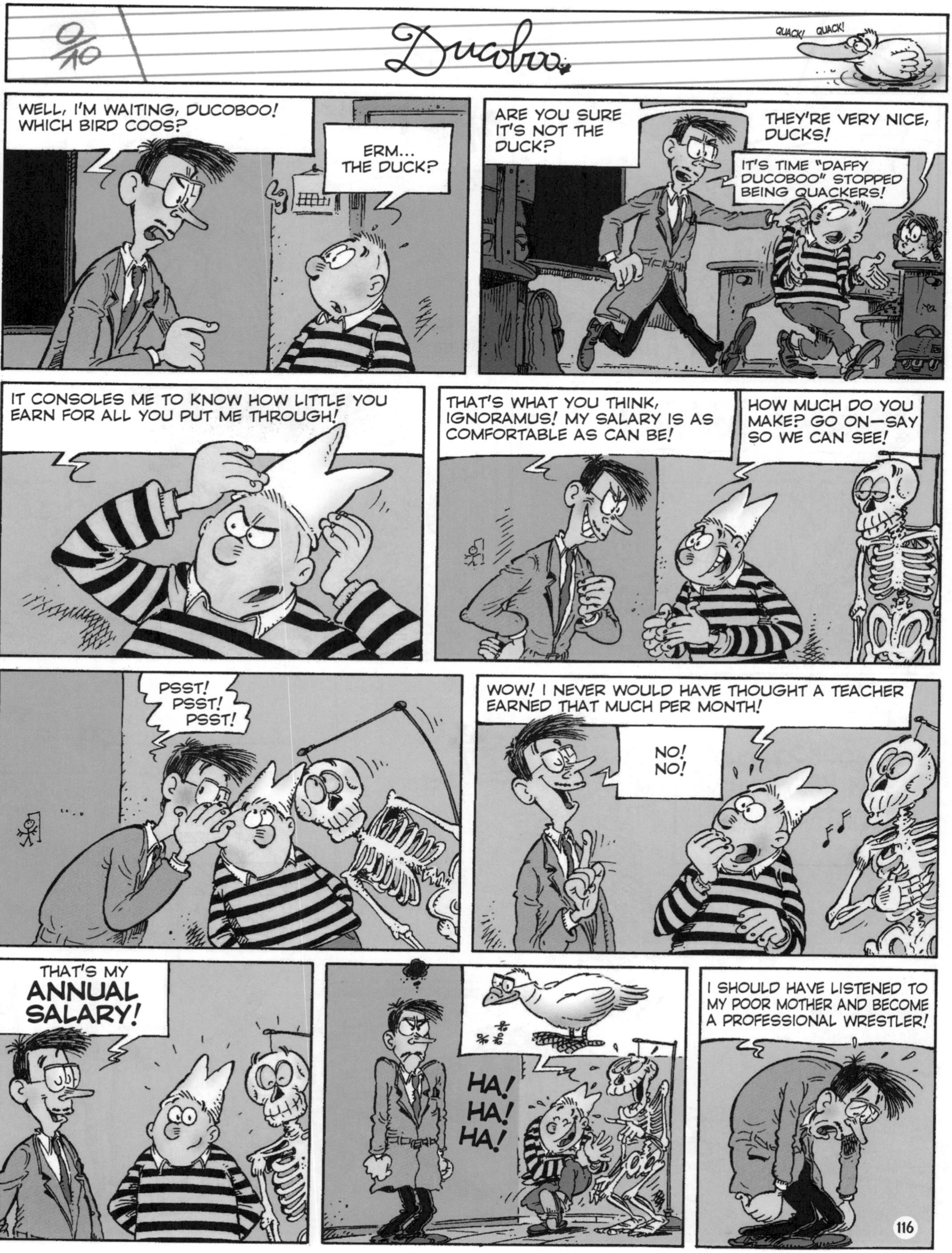

Ducoboo
QUACK! QUACK!
WELL, I'M WAITING, DUCOBOO! WHICH BIRD COOS?
ERM... THE DUCK?
ARE YOU SURE IT'S NOT THE DUCK?
THEY'RE VERY NICE, DUCKS!
IT'S TIME "DAFFY DUCOBOO" STOPPED BEING QUACKERS!
IT CONSOLES ME TO KNOW HOW LITTLE YOU EARN FOR ALL YOU PUT ME THROUGH!
THAT'S WHAT YOU THINK, IGNORAMUS! MY SALARY IS AS COMFORTABLE AS CAN BE!
HOW MUCH DO YOU MAKE? GO ON—SAY SO WE CAN SEE!
PSST! PSST! PSST!
WOW! I NEVER WOULD HAVE THOUGHT A TEACHER EARNED THAT MUCH PER MONTH!
NO! NO!
THAT'S MY ANNUAL SALARY!
HA! HA! HA!
I SHOULD HAVE LISTENED TO MY POOR MOTHER AND BECOME A PROFESSIONAL WRESTLER!
116

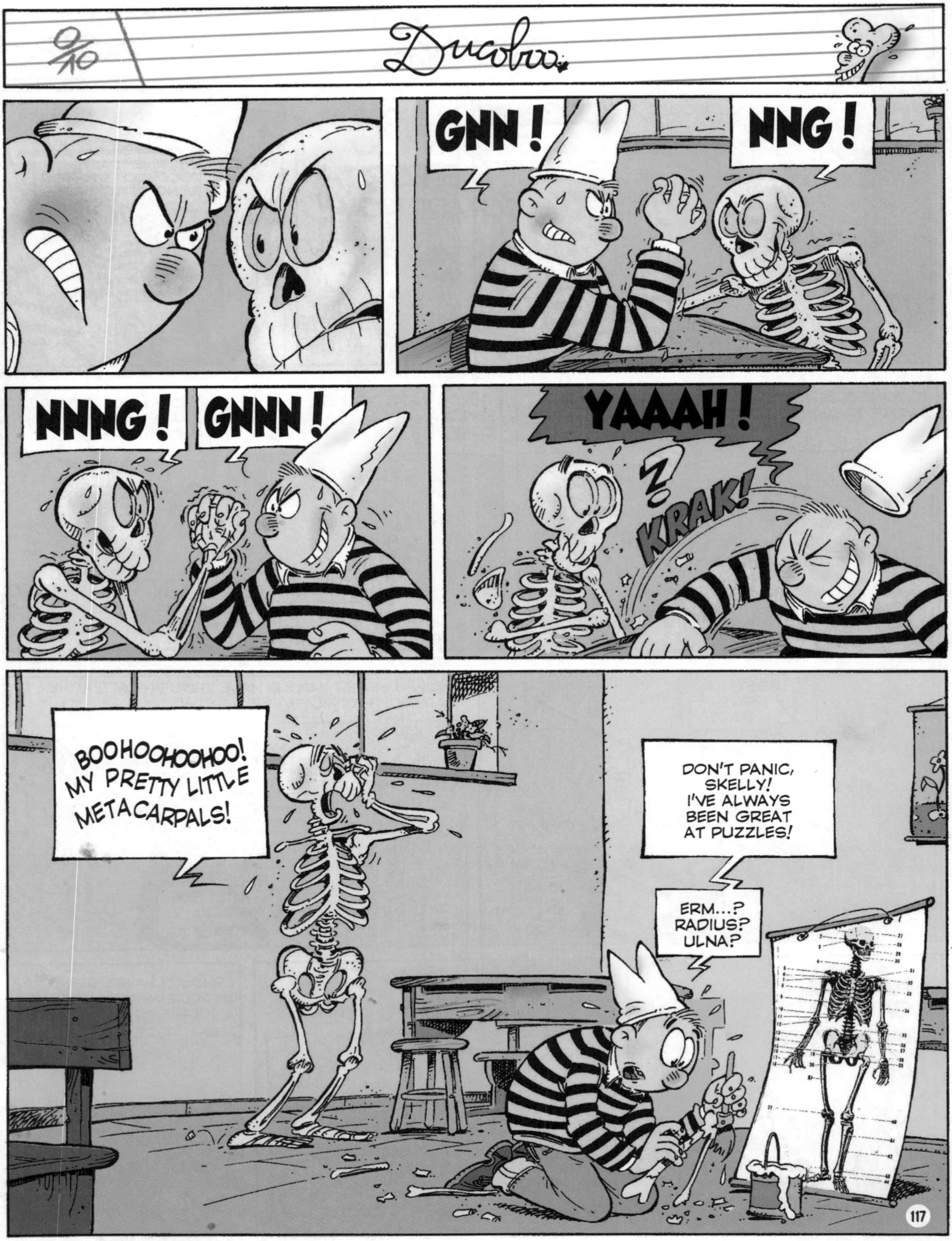

Ducobu
0/10
GNN!
NNG!
NNNG!
GNNN!
YAAAH!
KRAK!
BOOHOOHOOHOO! MY PRETTY LITTLE METACARPALS!
DON'T PANIC, SKELLY! I'VE ALWAYS BEEN GREAT AT PUZZLES!
ERM...? RADIUS? ULNA?
117

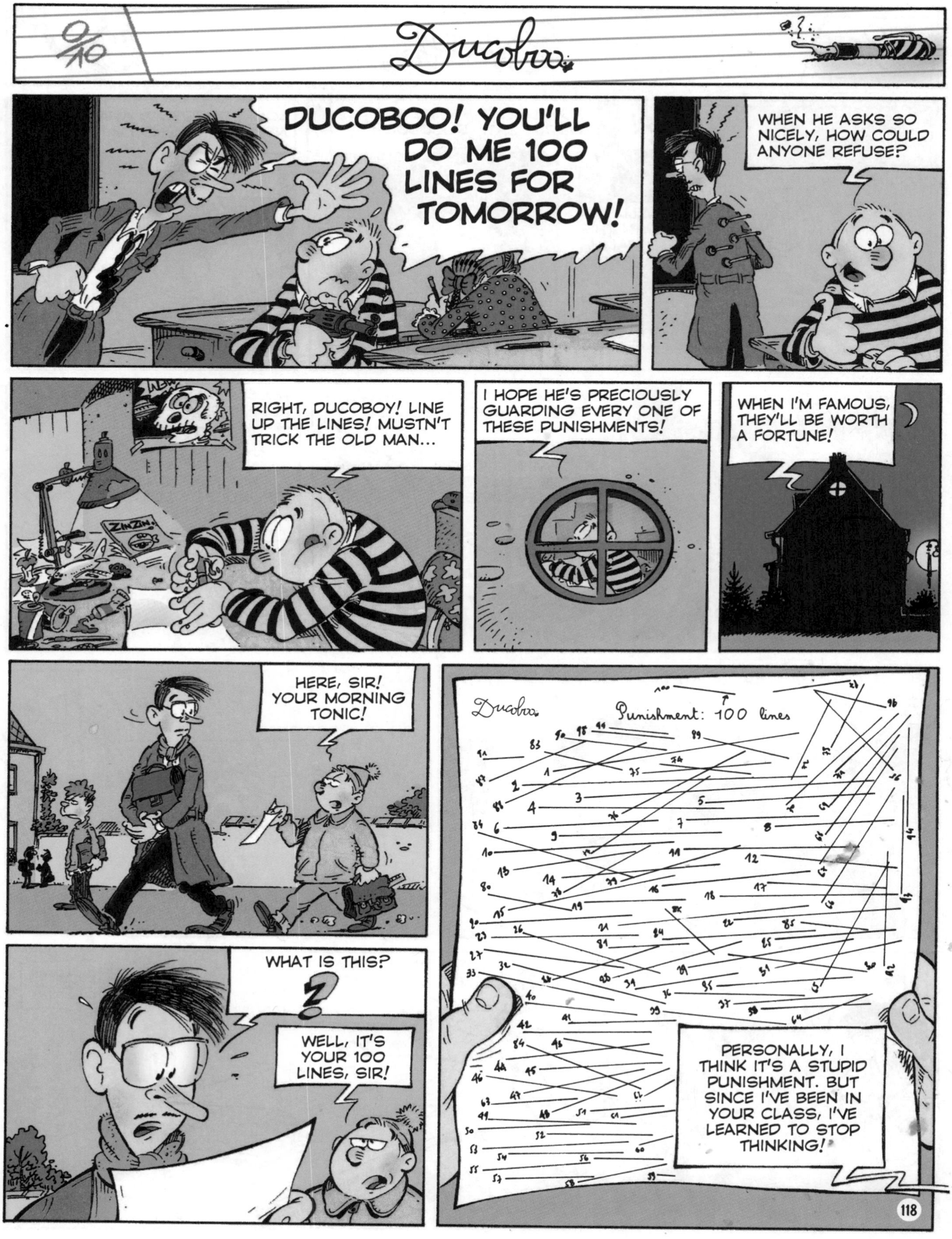
0/10
Ducoboo
DUCOBOO! YOU'LL DO ME 100 LINES FOR TOMORROW!
WHEN HE ASKS SO NICELY, HOW COULD ANYONE REFUSE?
RIGHT, DUCOBOY! LINE UP THE LINES! MUSTN'T TRICK THE OLD MAN...
ZINZIN
I HOPE HE'S PRECIOUSLY GUARDING EVERY ONE OF THESE PUNISHMENTS!
WHEN I'M FAMOUS, THEY'LL BE WORTH A FORTUNE!
HERE, SIR! YOUR MORNING TONIC!
Ducoboo
Punishment: 100 lines
WHAT IS THIS?
WELL, IT'S YOUR 100 LINES, SIR!
PERSONALLY, I THINK IT'S A STUPID PUNISHMENT. BUT SINCE I'VE BEEN IN YOUR CLASS, I'VE LEARNED TO STOP THINKING!
118

SINGULAR   PLURAL

Cat   Cat
            Boars
Goose

GULP!

HOW DID YOU WRITE THE WORD "CAT," DUCOBOO?

WELL, UH, WITH THIS CHALK!

LOOK, DUCOBOO, WHAT DO YOU NEED AT THE END OF "'CAT"?

A TAIL?

AN "S," DUCOBOO! AN "S"!

Cats
Boars

HOW DID I PROVOKE THE HEAVENS TO DESERVE SUCH A DUNCE?

HEY! LET ME TELL YOU THAT IT'S KIND OF YOUR FAULT THAT I'M IN THIS STATE!

HOLD ME BACK OR I'LL COMMIT PUPILICIDE!!

AND YOU SHOULD KNOW, SIIIIR, THAT VIOLENCE ONLY PRODUCES MEDIOCRE TEACHING RESULTS!

CRAK

THERE, THERE! MY GOOD LATOUCHE! JUST THINK, THE HOLIDAYS ARE COMING IN A FEW MONTHS!

MIAWWW!

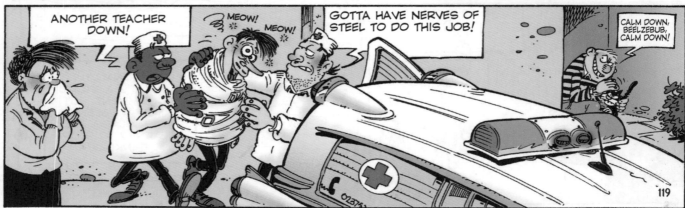

ANOTHER TEACHER DOWN!

MEOW!   MEOW!

GOTTA HAVE NERVES OF STEEL TO DO THIS JOB!

CALM DOWN, BEELZEBUB, CALM DOWN!

119

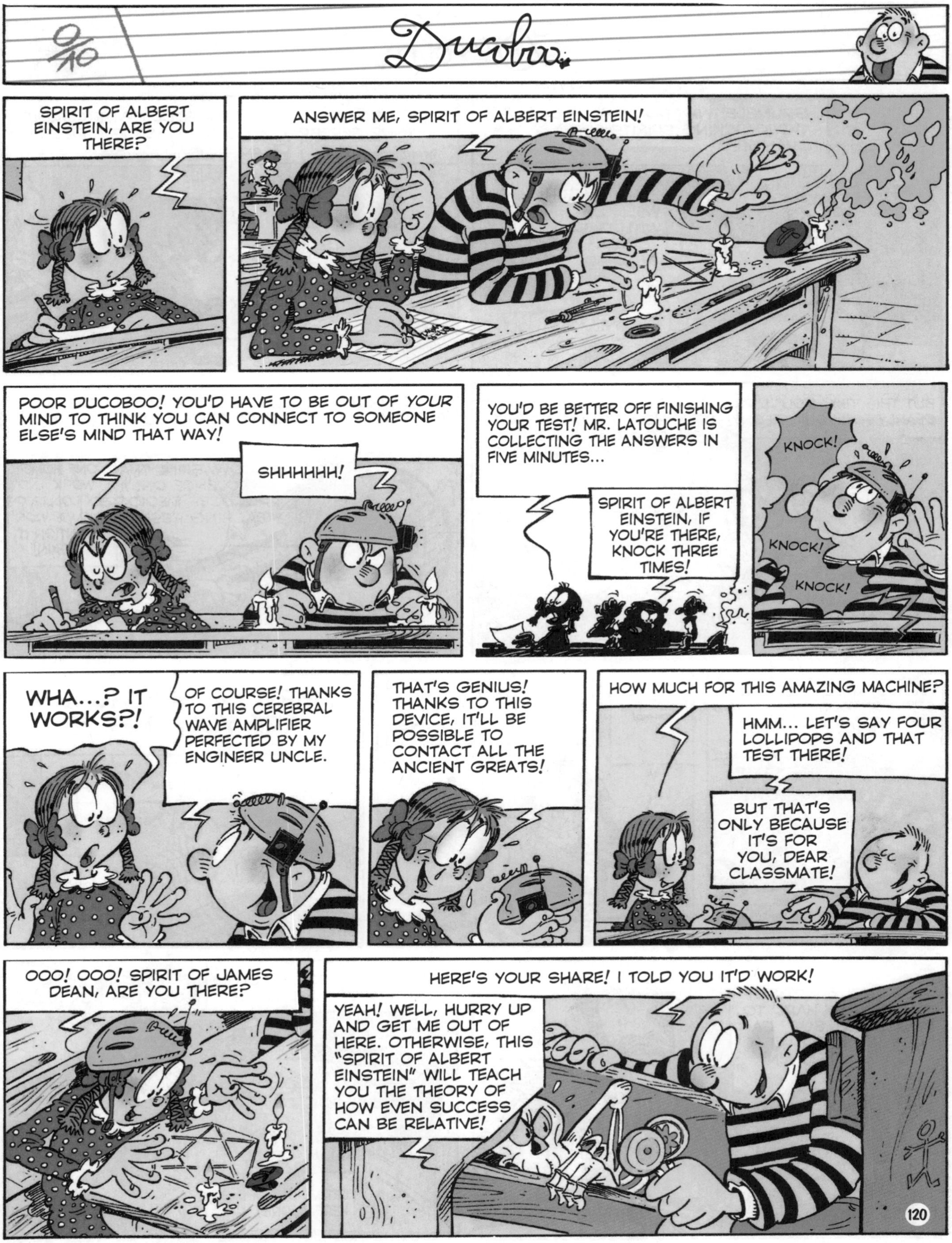

0/10
Ducoboo
SPIRIT OF ALBERT EINSTEIN, ARE YOU THERE?
ANSWER ME, SPIRIT OF ALBERT EINSTEIN!
POOR DUCOBOO! YOU'D HAVE TO BE OUT OF *YOUR* MIND TO THINK YOU CAN CONNECT TO SOMEONE ELSE'S MIND THAT WAY!
SHHHHHH!
YOU'D BE BETTER OFF FINISHING YOUR TEST! MR. LATOUCHE IS COLLECTING THE ANSWERS IN FIVE MINUTES...
SPIRIT OF ALBERT EINSTEIN, IF YOU'RE THERE, KNOCK THREE TIMES!
KNOCK!
KNOCK!
KNOCK!
WHA...? IT WORKS?!
OF COURSE! THANKS TO THIS CEREBRAL WAVE AMPLIFIER PERFECTED BY MY ENGINEER UNCLE.
THAT'S GENIUS! THANKS TO THIS DEVICE, IT'LL BE POSSIBLE TO CONTACT ALL THE ANCIENT GREATS!
HOW MUCH FOR THIS AMAZING MACHINE?
HMM... LET'S SAY FOUR LOLLIPOPS AND THAT TEST THERE!
BUT THAT'S ONLY BECAUSE IT'S FOR YOU, DEAR CLASSMATE!
OOO! OOO! SPIRIT OF JAMES DEAN, ARE YOU THERE?
HERE'S YOUR SHARE! I TOLD YOU IT'D WORK!
YEAH! WELL, HURRY UP AND GET ME OUT OF HERE. OTHERWISE, THIS "SPIRIT OF ALBERT EINSTEIN" WILL TEACH YOU THE THEORY OF HOW EVEN SUCCESS CAN BE RELATIVE!
120

GRUMBLE! WHY DON'T YOU PLAYING THE KNOCKING SPIRITS FOR A CHANGE?

SHH! HERE SHE IS!

DUCOBOO, YOU'VE MADE A FOOL OF ME AGAIN! YOUR CEREBRAL WAVE AMPLIFIER IS A PIECE OF 🌀💢🐛🗯️✨

VLAM!

BUT THIS TIME, YOU'LL PAY DEARLY FOR YOUR FELONY!

OF COURSE, IF THAT'S HOW YOU'RE GOING TO TREAT THESE FRAGILE MECHANICS! LET ME HAVE A LOOK AT IT!

I SEE WHAT IT IS: JUST A LITTLE SNAG HERE. NO BIG DEAL. IT SHOULDN'T COST YOU TOO MUCH...

LET'S SAY ONE HOMEWORK AND SIX LOLLIPOPS AND WE WON'T MENTION IT AGAIN!

I'LL TEST IT OUT RIGHT NOW. SPIRIT OF BEETHOVEN, IF YOU ARE THERE, KNOCK THREE TIMES!

NOTHING!

HEH HEH! THEY DO SAY THE OLD FELLA WAS A LITTLE HARD OF HEARING.

SPIRIT OF BEETHOVEN, ARE YOU THERE?

DON'T BE AN IDIOT, SPIRIT OF BEETHOVEN!

THE SPIRIT OF MATE HOVEN WANTS HIS SHARE OF THE LOOT INCREASED!

OBVIOUSLY, WITHOUT THE HAIR I'M HARD TO RECOGNISE, BUT I CAN ASSURE YOU THAT IT IS I, MATE HOVEN!

DOH!

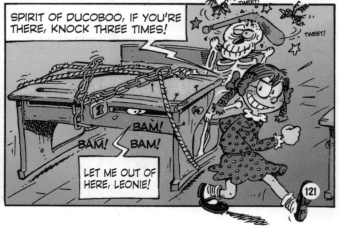

SPIRIT OF DUCOBOO, IF YOU'RE THERE, KNOCK THREE TIMES!

TWEET!

TWEET!

BAM! BAM! BAM! BAM!

LET ME OUT OF HERE, LEONIE!

121

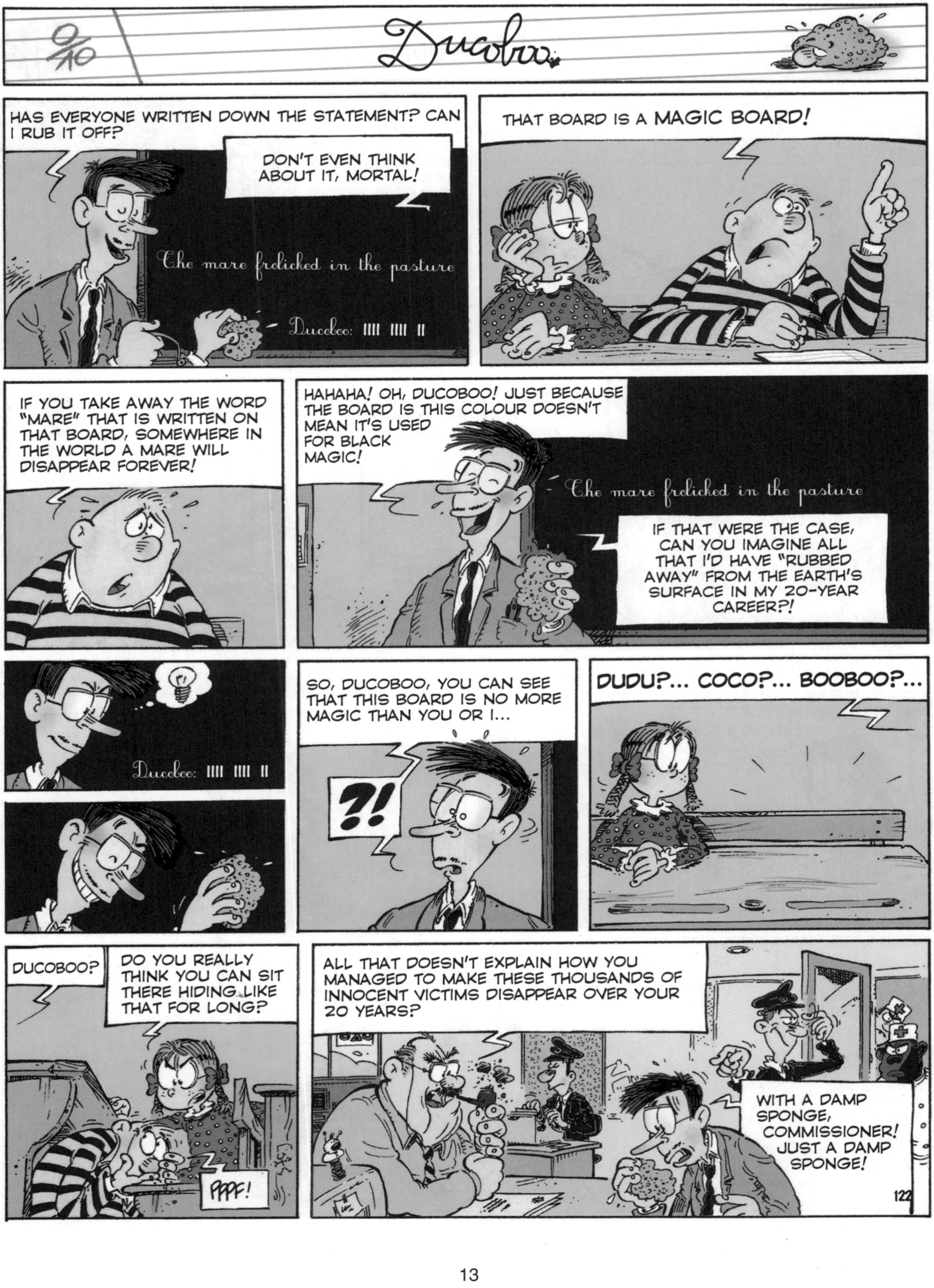
9/10
Ducoboo
HAS EVERYONE WRITTEN DOWN THE STATEMENT? CAN I RUB IT OFF?
DON'T EVEN THINK ABOUT IT, MORTAL!
The mare frolicked in the pasture
Ducoboo: IIII IIII II
THAT BOARD IS A MAGIC BOARD!
IF YOU TAKE AWAY THE WORD "MARE" THAT IS WRITTEN ON THAT BOARD, SOMEWHERE IN THE WORLD A MARE WILL DISAPPEAR FOREVER!
HAHAHA! OH, DUCOBOO! JUST BECAUSE THE BOARD IS THIS COLOUR DOESN'T MEAN IT'S USED FOR BLACK MAGIC!
The mare frolicked in the pasture
IF THAT WERE THE CASE, CAN YOU IMAGINE ALL THAT I'D HAVE "RUBBED AWAY" FROM THE EARTH'S SURFACE IN MY 20-YEAR CAREER?!
Ducoboo: IIII IIII II
SO, DUCOBOO, YOU CAN SEE THAT THIS BOARD IS NO MORE MAGIC THAN YOU OR I...
?!
DUDU?... COCO?... BOOBOO?...
DUCOBOO?
DO YOU REALLY THINK YOU CAN SIT THERE HIDING LIKE THAT FOR LONG?
PFFF!
ALL THAT DOESN'T EXPLAIN HOW YOU MANAGED TO MAKE THESE THOUSANDS OF INNOCENT VICTIMS DISAPPEAR OVER YOUR 20 YEARS?
WITH A DAMP SPONGE, COMMISSIONER! JUST A DAMP SPONGE!
122

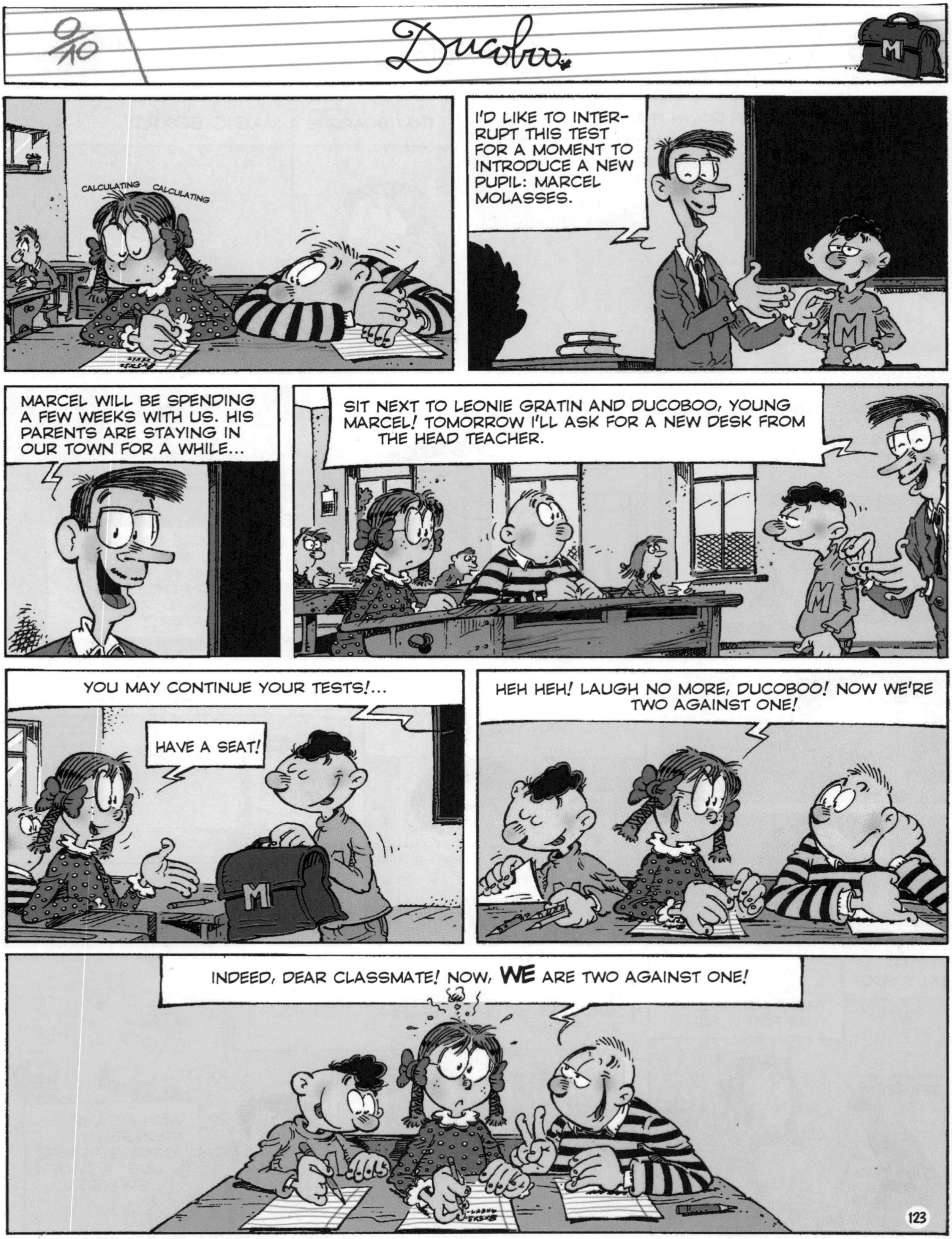
Ducoboo
9/10
CALCULATING CALCULATING
I'D LIKE TO INTERRUPT THIS TEST FOR A MOMENT TO INTRODUCE A NEW PUPIL: MARCEL MOLASSES.
MARCEL WILL BE SPENDING A FEW WEEKS WITH US. HIS PARENTS ARE STAYING IN OUR TOWN FOR A WHILE...
SIT NEXT TO LEONIE GRATIN AND DUCOBOO, YOUNG MARCEL! TOMORROW I'LL ASK FOR A NEW DESK FROM THE HEAD TEACHER.
YOU MAY CONTINUE YOUR TESTS!...
HAVE A SEAT!
HEH HEH! LAUGH NO MORE, DUCOBOO! NOW WE'RE TWO AGAINST ONE!
INDEED, DEAR CLASSMATE! NOW, **WE** ARE TWO AGAINST ONE!
123

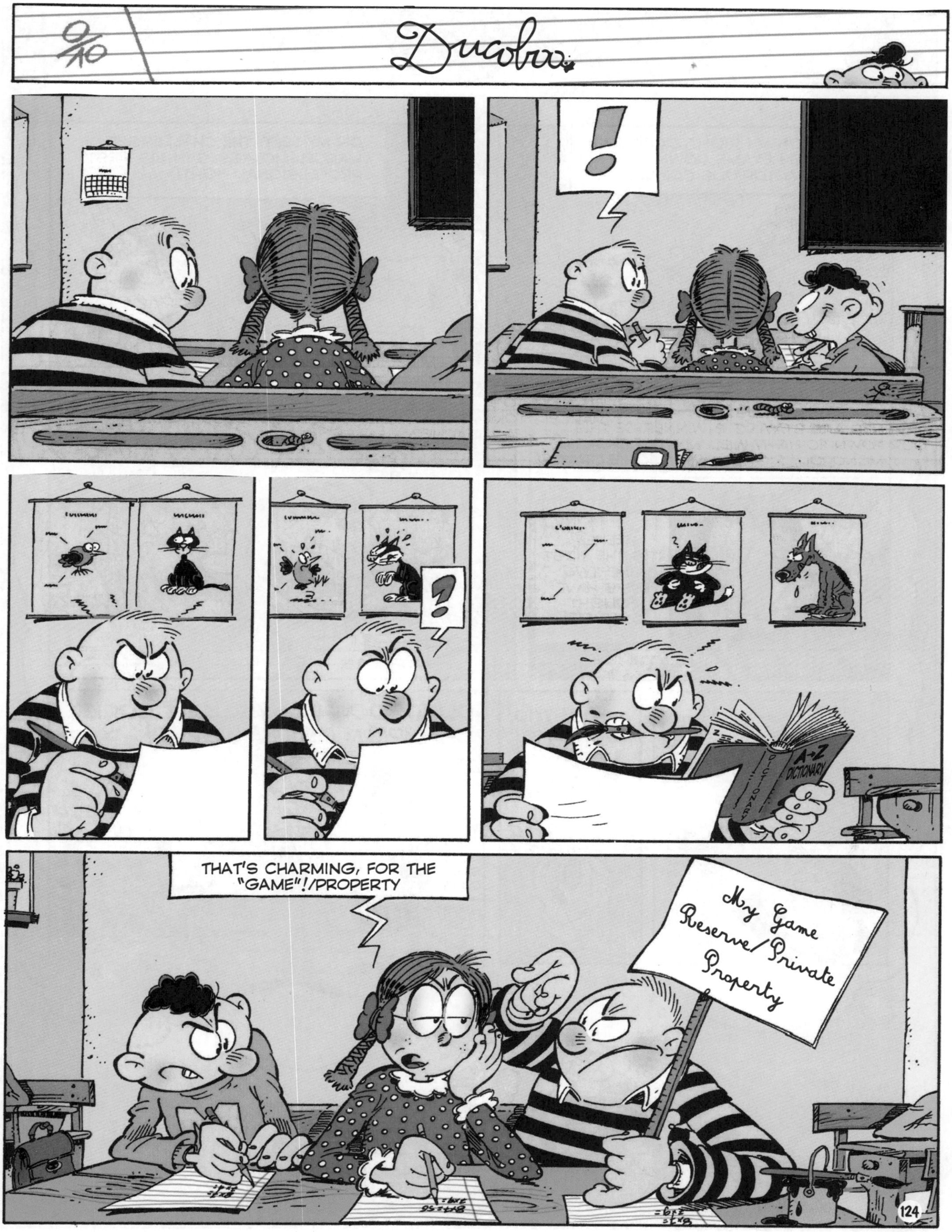

Ducobu
!
!
A-Z DICTIONARY
THAT'S CHARMING, FOR THE "GAME"!/PROPERTY
My Game Reserve/Private Property
124

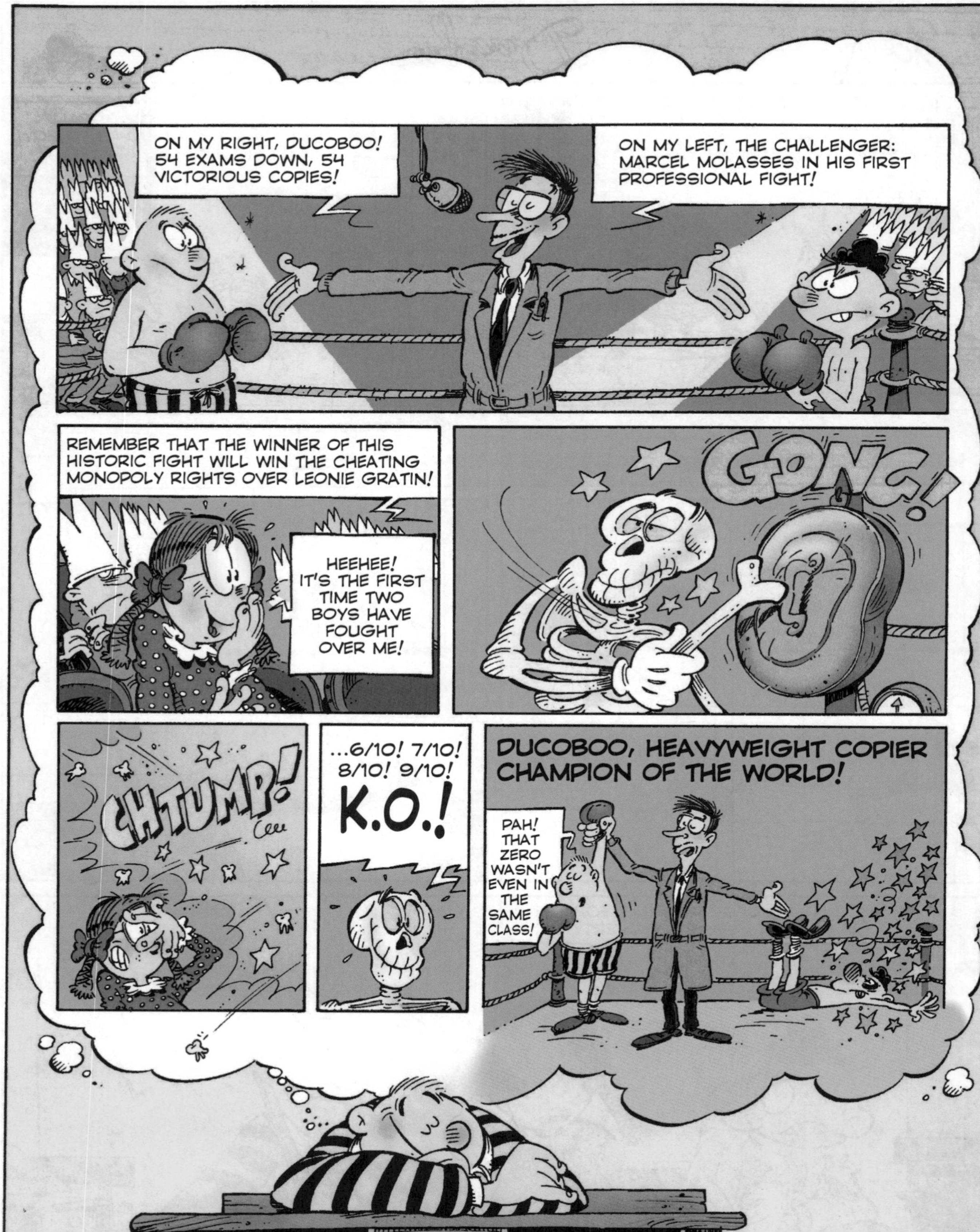

ON MY RIGHT, DUCOBOO! 54 EXAMS DOWN, 54 VICTORIOUS COPIES!
ON MY LEFT, THE CHALLENGER: MARCEL MOLASSES IN HIS FIRST PROFESSIONAL FIGHT!
REMEMBER THAT THE WINNER OF THIS HISTORIC FIGHT WILL WIN THE CHEATING MONOPOLY RIGHTS OVER LEONIE GRATIN!
HEEHEE! IT'S THE FIRST TIME TWO BOYS HAVE FOUGHT OVER ME!
GONG!
CHTUMP!
...6/10! 7/10! 8/10! 9/10!
K.O.!
DUCOBOO, HEAVYWEIGHT COPIER CHAMPION OF THE WORLD!
PAH! THAT ZERO WASN'T EVEN IN THE SAME CLASS!
125

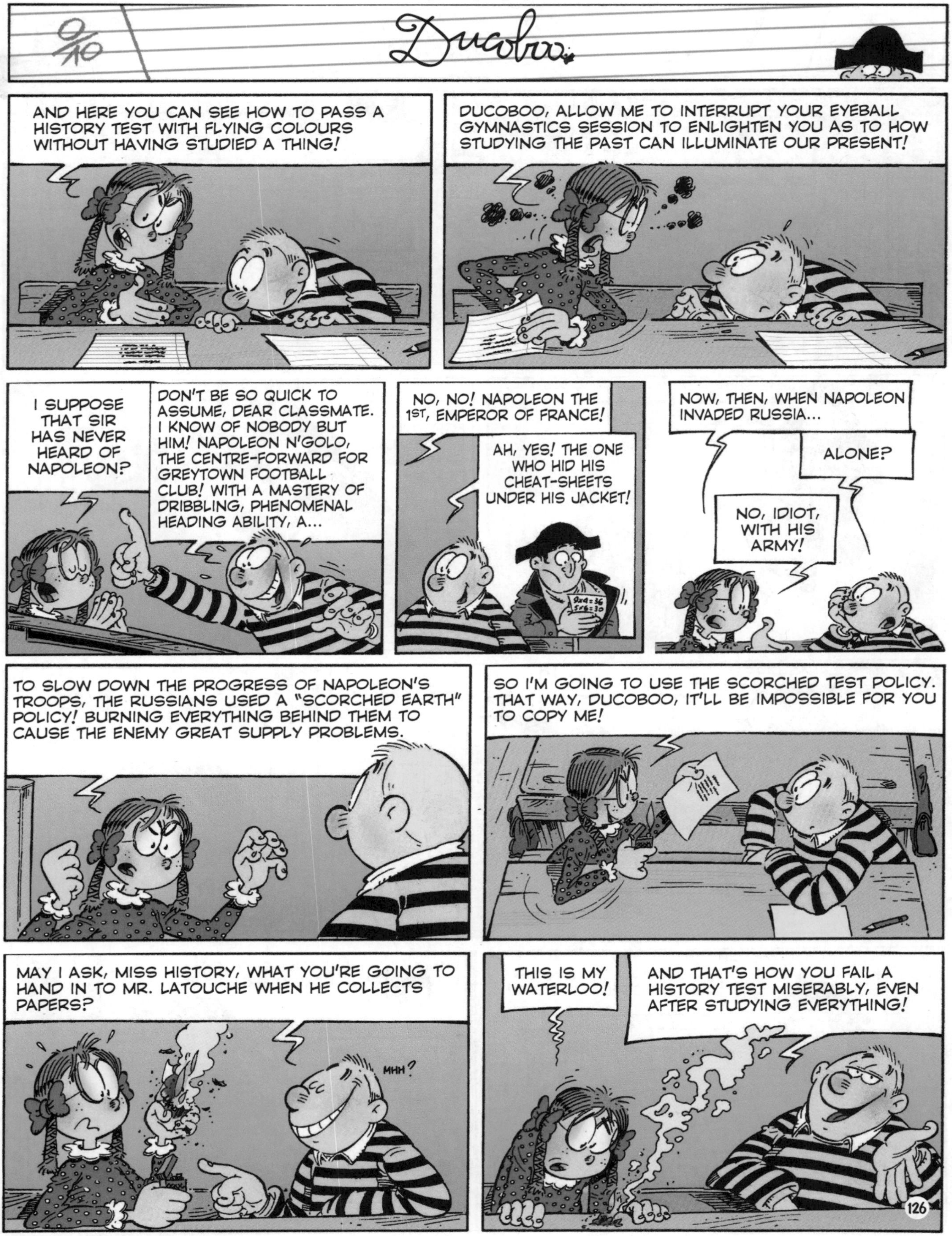
0/10
Ducoboo
AND HERE YOU CAN SEE HOW TO PASS A HISTORY TEST WITH FLYING COLOURS WITHOUT HAVING STUDIED A THING!
DUCOBOO, ALLOW ME TO INTERRUPT YOUR EYEBALL GYMNASTICS SESSION TO ENLIGHTEN YOU AS TO HOW STUDYING THE PAST CAN ILLUMINATE OUR PRESENT!
I SUPPOSE THAT SIR HAS NEVER HEARD OF NAPOLEON?
DON'T BE SO QUICK TO ASSUME, DEAR CLASSMATE. I KNOW OF NOBODY BUT HIM! NAPOLEON N'GOLO, THE CENTRE-FORWARD FOR GREYTOWN FOOTBALL CLUB! WITH A MASTERY OF DRIBBLING, PHENOMENAL HEADING ABILITY, A...
NO, NO! NAPOLEON THE 1ST, EMPEROR OF FRANCE!
AH, YES! THE ONE WHO HID HIS CHEAT-SHEETS UNDER HIS JACKET!
NOW, THEN, WHEN NAPOLEON INVADED RUSSIA...
ALONE?
NO, IDIOT, WITH HIS ARMY!
TO SLOW DOWN THE PROGRESS OF NAPOLEON'S TROOPS, THE RUSSIANS USED A "SCORCHED EARTH" POLICY! BURNING EVERYTHING BEHIND THEM TO CAUSE THE ENEMY GREAT SUPPLY PROBLEMS.
SO I'M GOING TO USE THE SCORCHED TEST POLICY. THAT WAY, DUCOBOO, IT'LL BE IMPOSSIBLE FOR YOU TO COPY ME!
MAY I ASK, MISS HISTORY, WHAT YOU'RE GOING TO HAND IN TO MR. LATOUCHE WHEN HE COLLECTS PAPERS?
MHH?
THIS IS MY WATERLOO!
AND THAT'S HOW YOU FAIL A HISTORY TEST MISERABLY, EVEN AFTER STUDYING EVERYTHING!
126

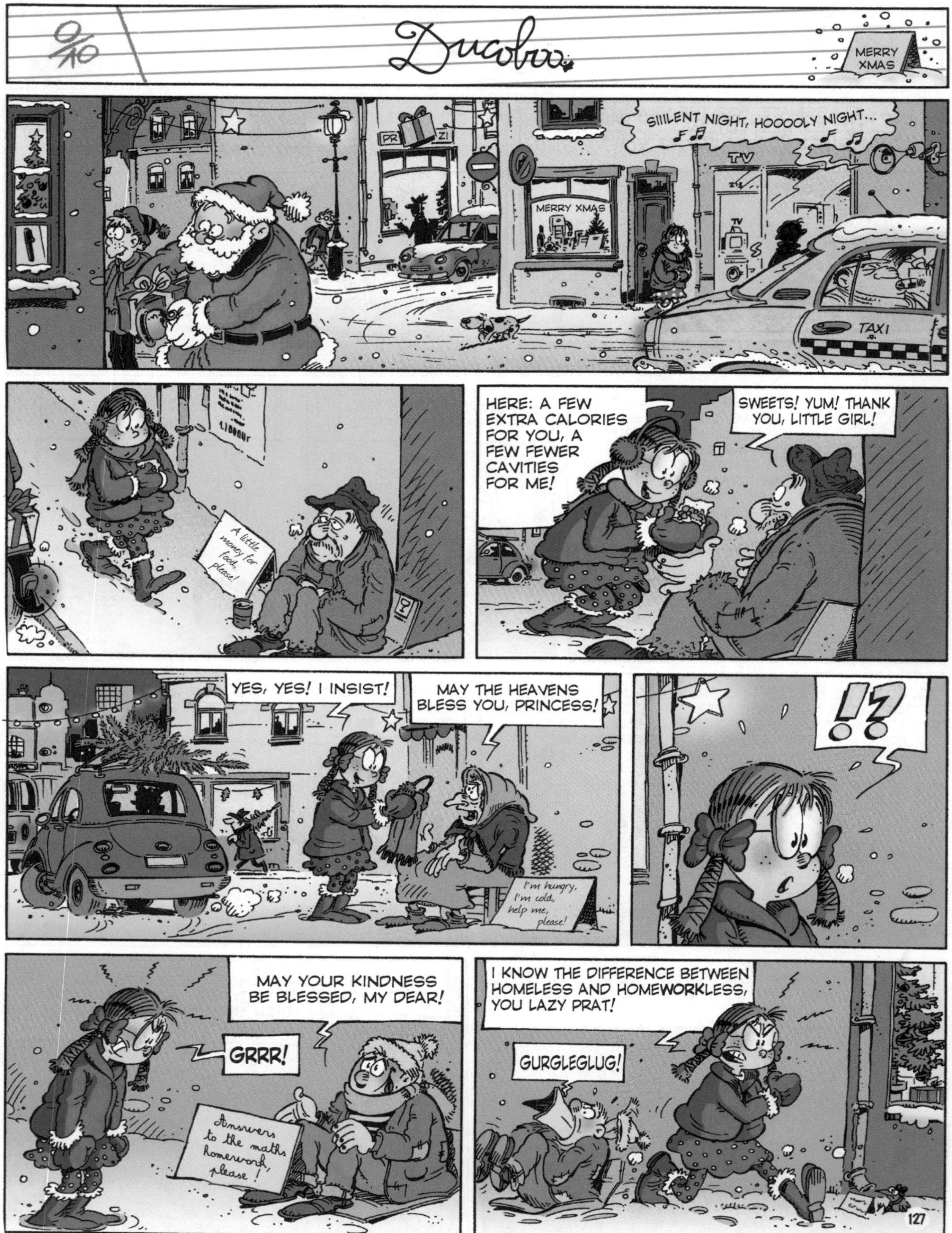
0/10
Ducobu
MERRY XMAS
SIIILENT NIGHT, HOOOOLY NIGHT...
MERRY XMAS
TV
TAXI
A little money for food, please!
HERE: A FEW EXTRA CALORIES FOR YOU, A FEW FEWER CAVITIES FOR ME!
SWEETS! YUM! THANK YOU, LITTLE GIRL!
YES, YES! I INSIST!
MAY THE HEAVENS BLESS YOU, PRINCESS!
I'm hungry, I'm cold, help me, please!
!?
MAY YOUR KINDNESS BE BLESSED, MY DEAR!
GRRR!
Answers to the maths homework, please!
I KNOW THE DIFFERENCE BETWEEN HOMELESS AND HOMEWORKLESS, YOU LAZY PRAT!
GURGLEGLUG!
127

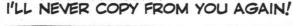

DEAR CLASSMATE, FOR THE NEW YEAR I HAVE MADE A RESOLUTION:
I'LL NEVER COPY FROM YOU AGAIN!

HAHAHA! GIVE ME A BREAK! THE REPENTING COPIER... YOU'VE DONE THAT ONE BEFORE!

ONCE A CHEATER, ALWAYS A CHEATER!

!

GO ON! JUST A LITTLE ANSWER!

AS THE BANTU PROVERB SAYS, "IF YOU GIVE A CORRECT ANSWER TO A COPIER, HE'LL GET 10 OUT OF 10 FOR A DAY. IF YOU TEACH HIM TO STUDY, HE'LL GET 10 OUT OF 10 FOR THE REST OF HIS LIFE!"

TAKE IT AND COPY! THESE ARE MY ANSWERS, GIVEN UP FOR YOU!

A RESOLUTION'S A RESOLUTION!

YOU WILL COPY OFF ME. SAY IT!!?

YOU WILL COPY OFF ME?!

BOOHOO! HE NEVER EVEN GLANCES AT MY PAPER ANYMORE! SNIFF!

THERE, THERE! IT'LL PASS, YOU'LL SEE!...

SNIFF

SNIFF

128

GOSSIP CENTRAL

INCREDIBLE
DUCOBOO HAS MADE THE RESOLUTION TO STOP COPYING OFF LEONIE GRATIN

Ducoboo refusing Leonie Gratin's advances. Who would have thought they'd witness this surreal scene? The New York Stock Exchange reacted immediately to this amazing story; dunce hat stocks fell several points to reach their lowest levels in 20 years!

"I've tried everything to make him see sense, but nothing works!" said Leonie Gratin, clearly not at her best. "Already for the last few weeks, Ducoboo has stopped copying off me completely. In these conditions, you understand, it's no longer any fun to be top of the class!"

Sceptical!

Ducoboo's classroom leader, Mr. Latouche, has declared that he is as sceptical as can be. "Ducoboo has copied Leonie Gratin since his earliest years. He was born the same year, the same day, the same time at the same minute as his desk-buddy. That's saying something! No, really, I don't think that this parasite is capable of keeping his fantastical resolution!"

Worried!

Skelly, Ducoboo's corner brother, couldn't hide his concern either: "If Ducoboo won't copy anymore, he won't get in trouble. If he doesn't get in trouble, he won't come to the corner. If he doesn't come to the corner, whom will I play with then?"

We consulted Professor Baudet, a world-renowned Dunceologist, in order to find out if we should be worried about Ducoboo's spectacular turnaround. "We notice nowadays that dunces are swapping their dunce hats for mortarboards more and more. It's very troubling. For, you see, in our modern societies, the dunce incarnates the eternal unsubmissive, the rebel. A dunce who gives up and starts studying represents, thus, the death of a small part of the revolutionary in all of us!"

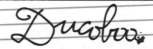 

DUCOBOO, IT'S BEEN NEARLY A MONTH SINCE YOU STOPPED COPYING OFF ME.

ONE MONTH THAT MY RIGHT ANSWERS AREN'T GOOD ENOUGH FOR YOU!

FOR PITY'S SAKE, DUCOBOO, BECOME THE CHEAT ELITE THAT EVERYONE LOVED SO MUCH!

OH! I KNOW WHAT YOU'LL TELL ME: "MISS GRATIN WAS NOT ALWAYS SO COOPERATIVE!"

IF ONLY YOU KNEW HOW MUCH I REGRET HAVING PUT AN EMBARGO ON YOU COPYING MY INEXHAUSTIBLE INTELLECTUAL RESOURCES!

I WAS A PRISONER OF MY REACTIONARY PRINCIPLES.

"WORK, TAKE PAINS; IT'S EFFORT THAT COSTS THE LEAST,"

"ALL WORK DESERVES A REWARD,"

AND SO ON AND SO FORTH!

I WAS LIKE A GARDENER GROWING BEAUTIFUL ROSES BUT NOT LETTING ANYONE ENJOY THE SCENT!

BUT I UNDERSTAND NOW: POSSESSION IS NOTHING, SHARING IS EVERYTHING!

AND, DUCOBOO, I WANT TO KNOW THE TRUTH!

GULP! IS THERE ANOTHER TOP-OF-THE-CLASS IN YOUR LIFE?

NO, BUT I REALLY THINK I'VE GOT A STIFF NECK!

OUCH!

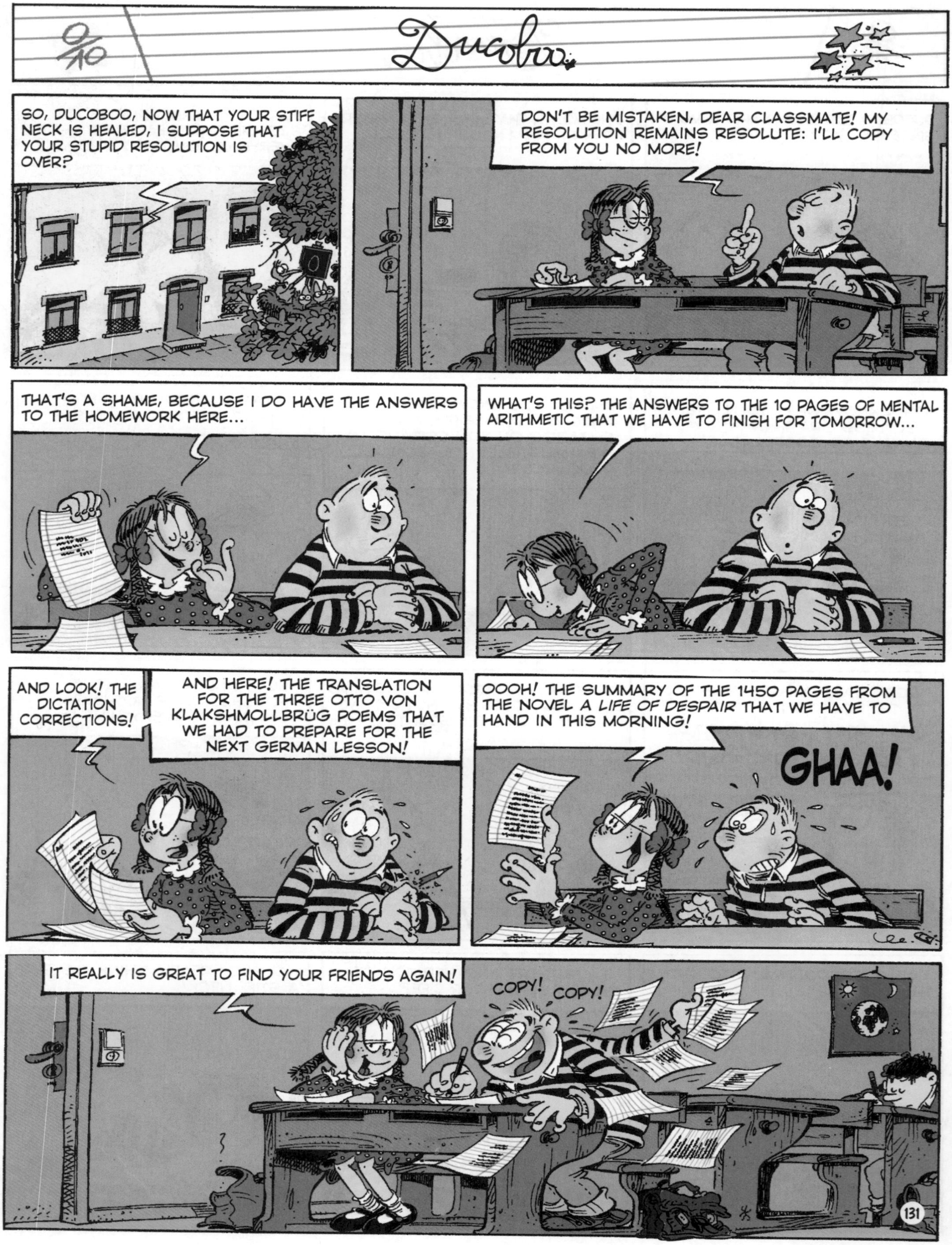
0/10
Ducoboo
131
SO, DUCOBOO, NOW THAT YOUR STIFF NECK IS HEALED, I SUPPOSE THAT YOUR STUPID RESOLUTION IS OVER?
DON'T BE MISTAKEN, DEAR CLASSMATE! MY RESOLUTION REMAINS RESOLUTE: I'LL COPY FROM YOU NO MORE!
THAT'S A SHAME, BECAUSE I DO HAVE THE ANSWERS TO THE HOMEWORK HERE...
WHAT'S THIS? THE ANSWERS TO THE 10 PAGES OF MENTAL ARITHMETIC THAT WE HAVE TO FINISH FOR TOMORROW...
AND LOOK! THE DICTATION CORRECTIONS!
AND HERE! THE TRANSLATION FOR THE THREE OTTO VON KLAKSHMOLLBRÜG POEMS THAT WE HAD TO PREPARE FOR THE NEXT GERMAN LESSON!
OOOH! THE SUMMARY OF THE 1450 PAGES FROM THE NOVEL A *LIFE OF DESPAIR* THAT WE HAVE TO HAND IN THIS MORNING!
GHAA!
IT REALLY IS GREAT TO FIND YOUR FRIENDS AGAIN!
COPY! COPY!

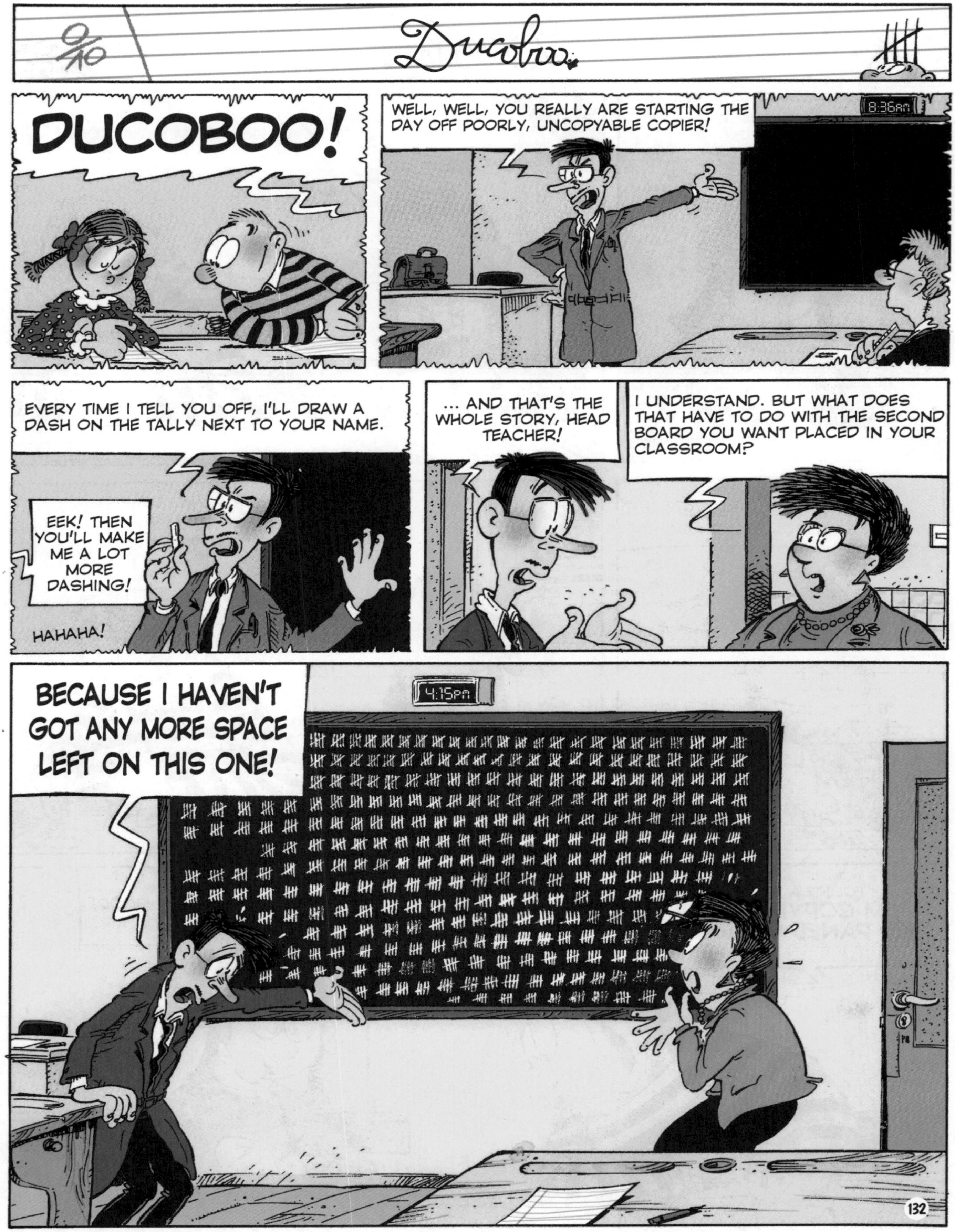

Ducoboo
0/10
DUCOBOO!
WELL, WELL, YOU REALLY ARE STARTING THE DAY OFF POORLY, UNCOPYABLE COPIER!
8:36am
EVERY TIME I TELL YOU OFF, I'LL DRAW A DASH ON THE TALLY NEXT TO YOUR NAME.
EEK! THEN YOU'LL MAKE ME A LOT MORE DASHING!
HAHAHA!
... AND THAT'S THE WHOLE STORY, HEAD TEACHER!
I UNDERSTAND. BUT WHAT DOES THAT HAVE TO DO WITH THE SECOND BOARD YOU WANT PLACED IN YOUR CLASSROOM?
BECAUSE I HAVEN'T GOT ANY MORE SPACE LEFT ON THIS ONE!
4:15pm
132

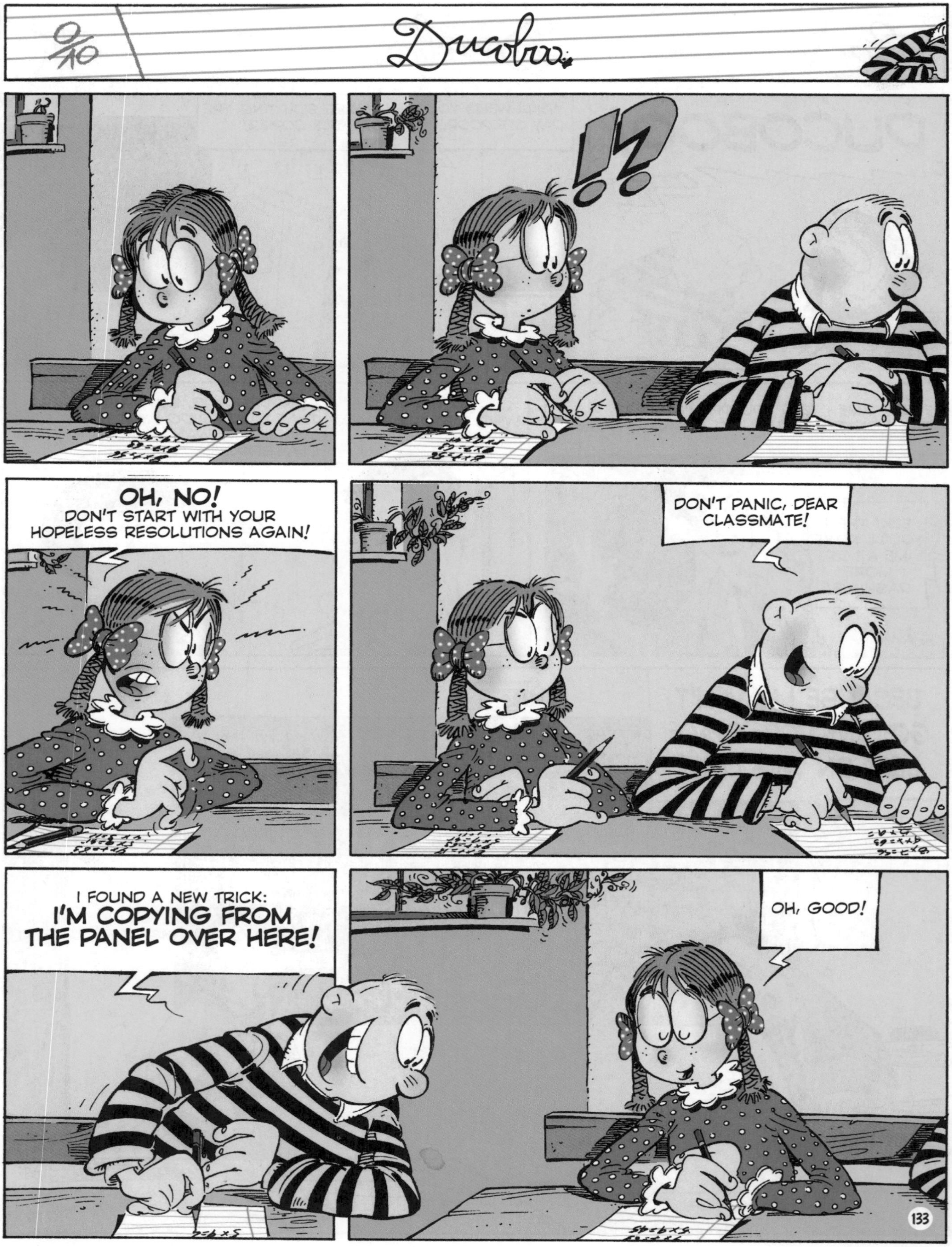

0/10
Ducobu
OH, NO! DON'T START WITH YOUR HOPELESS RESOLUTIONS AGAIN!
DON'T PANIC, DEAR CLASSMATE!
I FOUND A NEW TRICK: I'M COPYING FROM THE PANEL OVER HERE!
OH, GOOD!
133

WOW, DUCOBOO! WHAT DID YOU DO WITH YOUR HAIR?

IT'S THE NEW DO ABOUT TOWN.

IT'S CALLED THE "FULL HORNET."

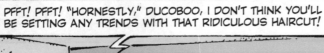

PFFT! PFFT! "HORNESTLY," DUCOBOO, I DON'T THINK YOU'LL BE SETTING ANY TRENDS WITH THAT RIDICULOUS HAIRCUT!

RIGHT! IT'S NOT GREAT, BUT I HAVE A TEST ON TIMES TABLES TO MEMORISE!

MEMORISE AWAY, DEAR CLASSMATE, MEMORISE!

PFFF!

THIS HAIRCUT SUITS YOU A LOT BETTER, DUCOBOO!

WE JUST HAVE TO GIVE IT A NAME!

WHAT DO YOU THINK OF, "THE ZERO OUT OF 10 BARNET"?

GRRR!!

134

25

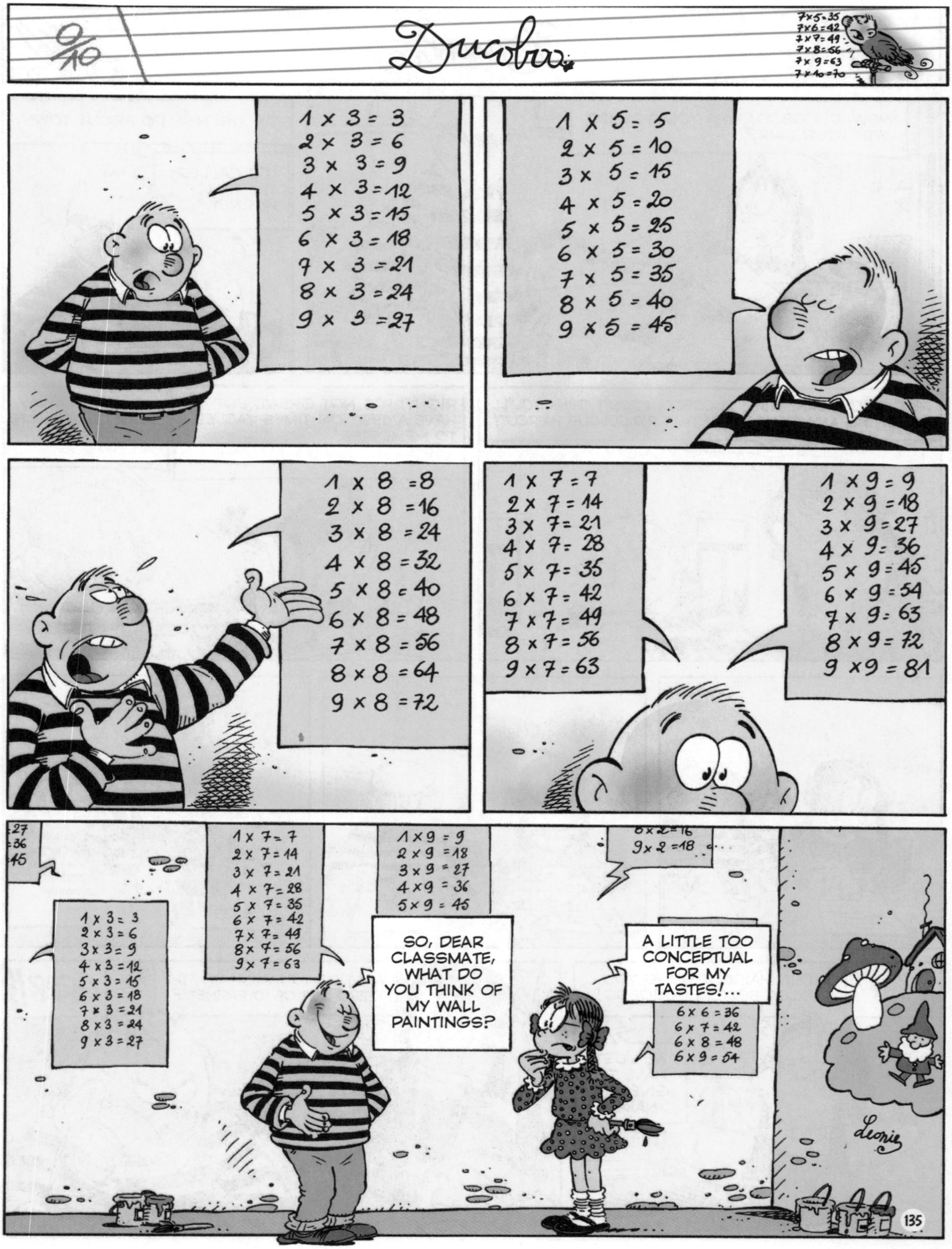
0/10
Ducobu
7×5=35
7×6=42
7×7=49
7×8=56
7×9=63
7×10=70
1 × 3 = 3
2 × 3 = 6
3 × 3 = 9
4 × 3 = 12
5 × 3 = 15
6 × 3 = 18
7 × 3 = 21
8 × 3 = 24
9 × 3 = 27
1 × 5 = 5
2 × 5 = 10
3 × 5 = 15
4 × 5 = 20
5 × 5 = 25
6 × 5 = 30
7 × 5 = 35
8 × 5 = 40
9 × 5 = 45
1 × 8 = 8
2 × 8 = 16
3 × 8 = 24
4 × 8 = 32
5 × 8 = 40
6 × 8 = 48
7 × 8 = 56
8 × 8 = 64
9 × 8 = 72
1 × 7 = 7
2 × 7 = 14
3 × 7 = 21
4 × 7 = 28
5 × 7 = 35
6 × 7 = 42
7 × 7 = 49
8 × 7 = 56
9 × 7 = 63
1 × 9 = 9
2 × 9 = 18
3 × 9 = 27
4 × 9 = 36
5 × 9 = 45
6 × 9 = 54
7 × 9 = 63
8 × 9 = 72
9 × 9 = 81
=27
=36
45
1 × 7 = 7
2 × 7 = 14
3 × 7 = 21
4 × 7 = 28
5 × 7 = 35
6 × 7 = 42
7 × 7 = 49
8 × 7 = 56
9 × 7 = 63
1 × 9 = 9
2 × 9 = 18
3 × 9 = 27
4 × 9 = 36
5 × 9 = 45
8 × 2 = 16
9 × 2 = 18
1 × 3 = 3
2 × 3 = 6
3 × 3 = 9
4 × 3 = 12
5 × 3 = 15
6 × 3 = 18
7 × 3 = 21
8 × 3 = 24
9 × 3 = 27
SO, DEAR CLASSMATE, WHAT DO YOU THINK OF MY WALL PAINTINGS?
A LITTLE TOO CONCEPTUAL FOR MY TASTES!...
6 × 6 = 36
6 × 7 = 42
6 × 8 = 48
6 × 9 = 54
Leonie
135

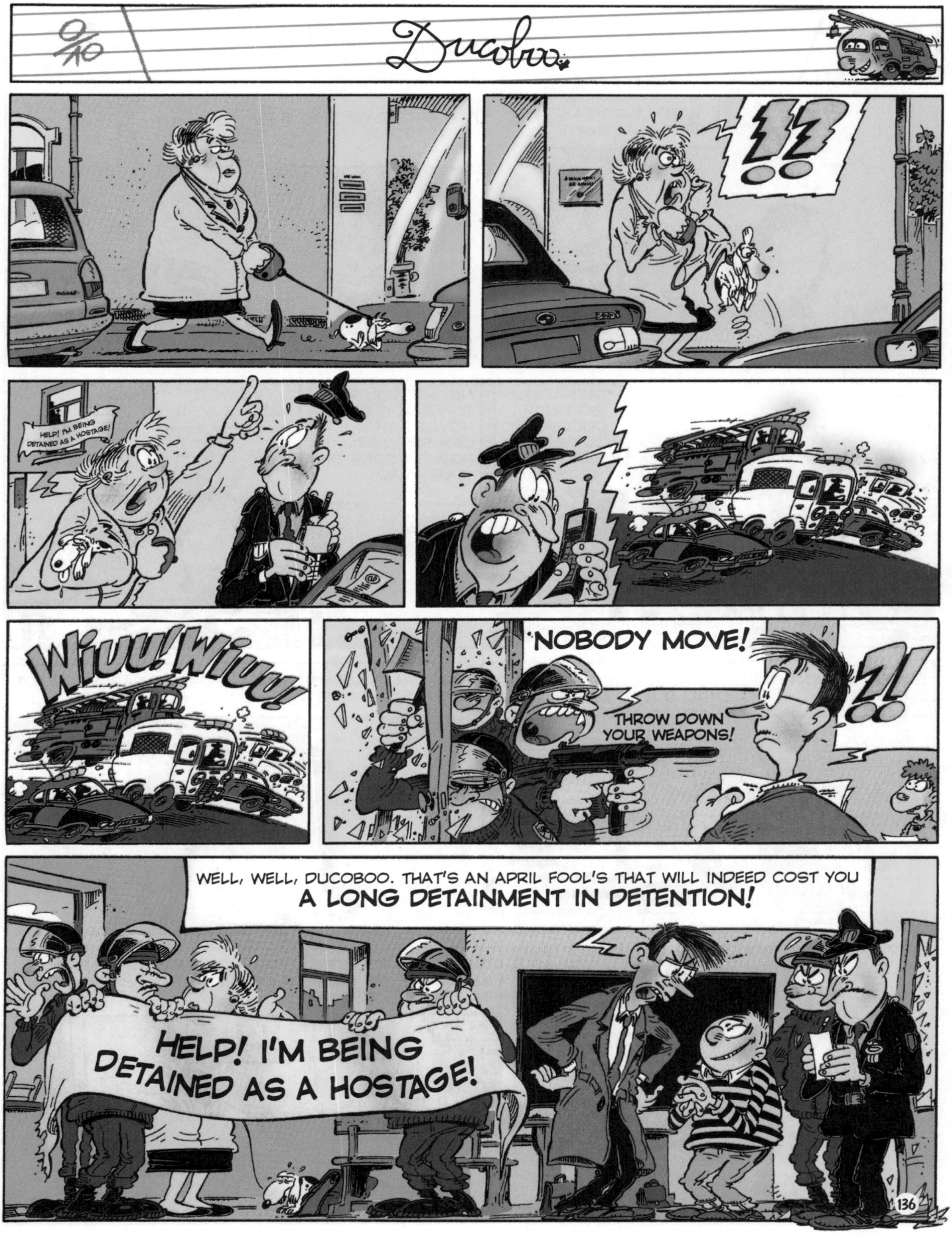
9/10
Ducoboo
!?
HELP! I'M BEING DETAINED AS A HOSTAGE!
WIUU! WIUU!
NOBODY MOVE!
THROW DOWN YOUR WEAPONS!
?!
WELL, WELL, DUCOBOO. THAT'S AN APRIL FOOL'S THAT WILL INDEED COST YOU A LONG DETAINMENT IN DETENTION!
HELP! I'M BEING DETAINED AS A HOSTAGE!
136

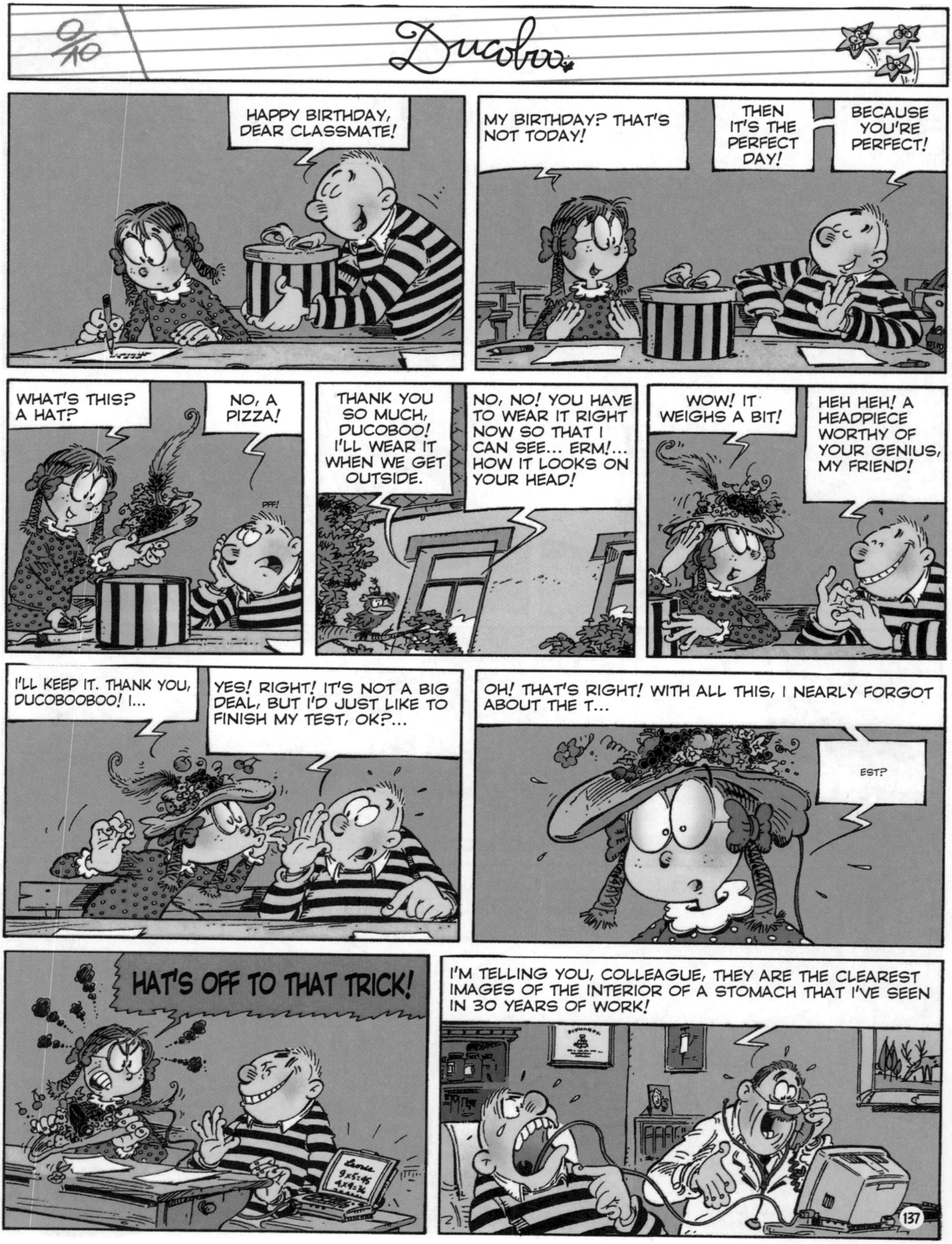
9/10
Ducoboo
HAPPY BIRTHDAY, DEAR CLASSMATE!
MY BIRTHDAY? THAT'S NOT TODAY!
THEN IT'S THE PERFECT DAY!
BECAUSE YOU'RE PERFECT!
WHAT'S THIS? A HAT?
NO, A PIZZA!
PFF!
THANK YOU SO MUCH, DUCOBOO! I'LL WEAR IT WHEN WE GET OUTSIDE.
NO, NO! YOU HAVE TO WEAR IT RIGHT NOW SO THAT I CAN SEE... ERM!... HOW IT LOOKS ON YOUR HEAD!
WOW! IT WEIGHS A BIT!
HEH HEH! A HEADPIECE WORTHY OF YOUR GENIUS, MY FRIEND!
I'LL KEEP IT. THANK YOU, DUCOBOOBOO! I...
YES! RIGHT! IT'S NOT A BIG DEAL, BUT I'D JUST LIKE TO FINISH MY TEST, OK?...
OH! THAT'S RIGHT! WITH ALL THIS, I NEARLY FORGOT ABOUT THE T...
EST?
HAT'S OFF TO THAT TRICK!
I'M TELLING YOU, COLLEAGUE, THEY ARE THE CLEAREST IMAGES OF THE INTERIOR OF A STOMACH THAT I'VE SEEN IN 30 YEARS OF WORK!
137

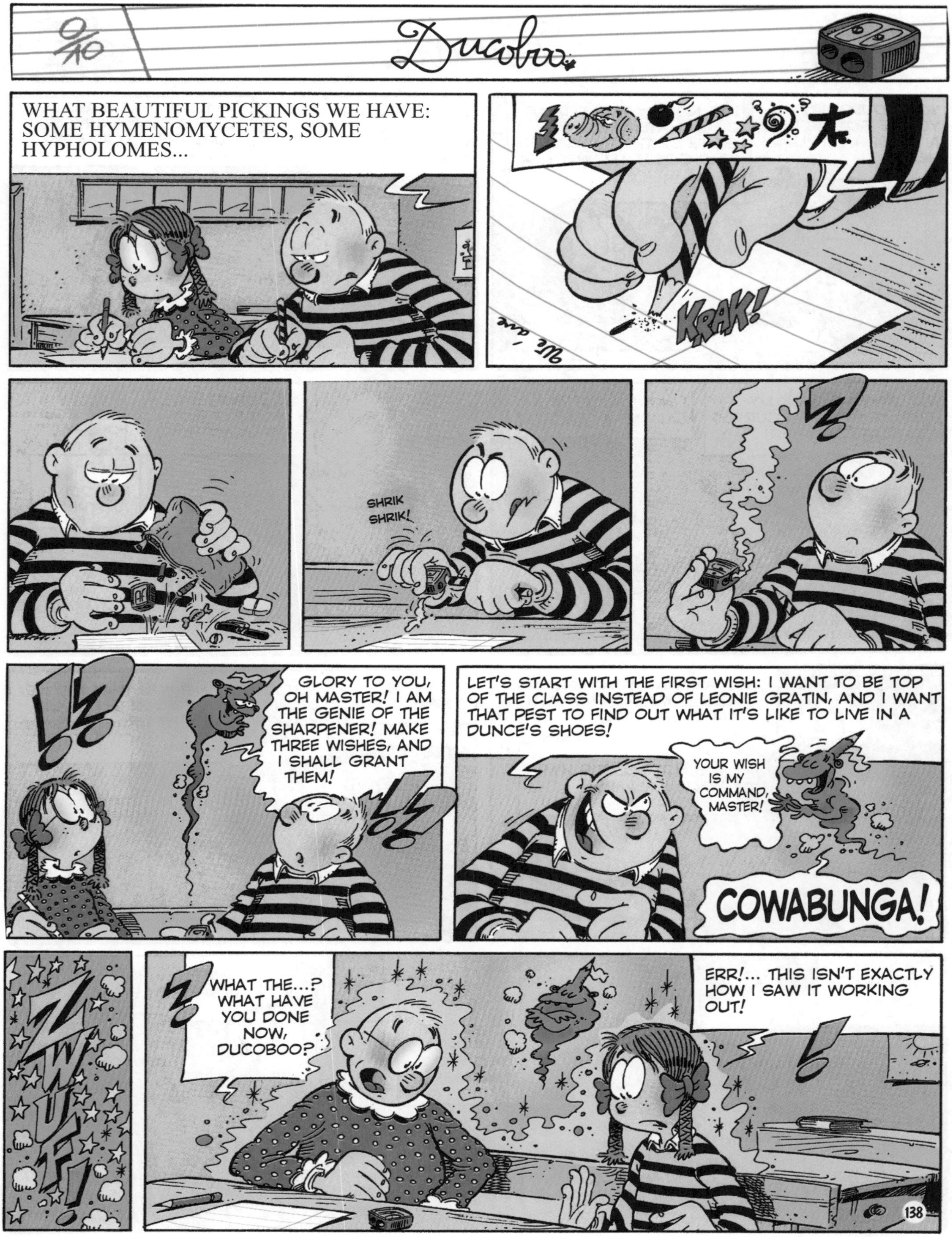
Ducoboo
WHAT BEAUTIFUL PICKINGS WE HAVE: SOME HYMENOMYCETES, SOME HYPHOLOMES...
KRAK!
SHRIK SHRIK!
GLORY TO YOU, OH MASTER! I AM THE GENIE OF THE SHARPENER! MAKE THREE WISHES, AND I SHALL GRANT THEM!
LET'S START WITH THE FIRST WISH: I WANT TO BE TOP OF THE CLASS INSTEAD OF LEONIE GRATIN, AND I WANT THAT PEST TO FIND OUT WHAT IT'S LIKE TO LIVE IN A DUNCE'S SHOES!
YOUR WISH IS MY COMMAND, MASTER!
COWABUNGA!
ZWUF!
WHAT THE...? WHAT HAVE YOU DONE NOW, DUCOBOO?
ERR!... THIS ISN'T EXACTLY HOW I SAW IT WORKING OUT!
138

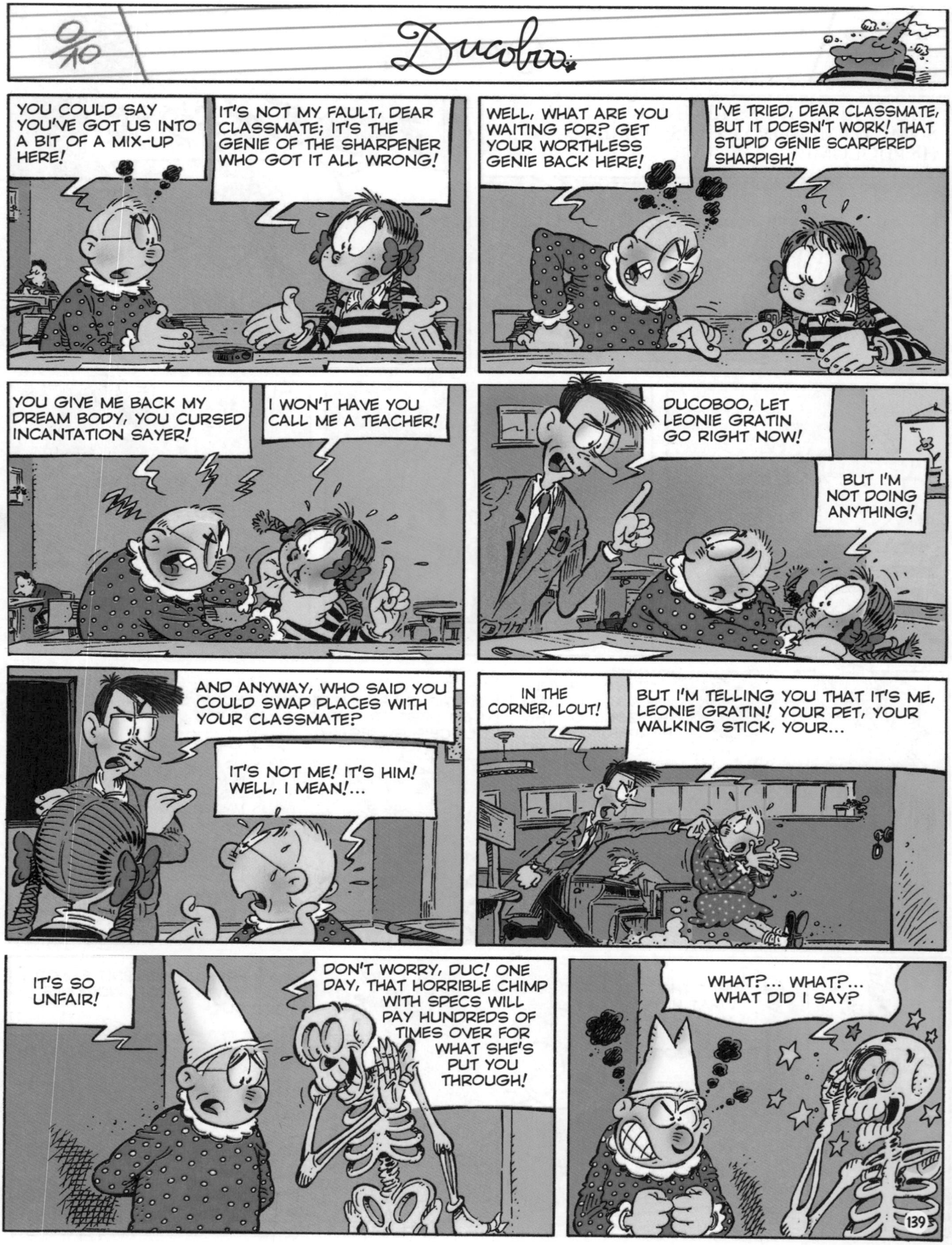
0/10
Ducoboo
YOU COULD SAY YOU'VE GOT US INTO A BIT OF A MIX-UP HERE!
IT'S NOT MY FAULT, DEAR CLASSMATE; IT'S THE GENIE OF THE SHARPENER WHO GOT IT ALL WRONG!
WELL, WHAT ARE YOU WAITING FOR? GET YOUR WORTHLESS GENIE BACK HERE!
I'VE TRIED, DEAR CLASSMATE, BUT IT DOESN'T WORK! THAT STUPID GENIE SCARPERED SHARPISH!
YOU GIVE ME BACK MY DREAM BODY, YOU CURSED INCANTATION SAYER!
I WON'T HAVE YOU CALL ME A TEACHER!
DUCOBOO, LET LEONIE GRATIN GO RIGHT NOW!
BUT I'M NOT DOING ANYTHING!
AND ANYWAY, WHO SAID YOU COULD SWAP PLACES WITH YOUR CLASSMATE?
IT'S NOT ME! IT'S HIM! WELL, I MEAN!...
IN THE CORNER, LOUT!
BUT I'M TELLING YOU THAT IT'S ME, LEONIE GRATIN! YOUR PET, YOUR WALKING STICK, YOUR...
IT'S SO UNFAIR!
DON'T WORRY, DUC! ONE DAY, THAT HORRIBLE CHIMP WITH SPECS WILL PAY HUNDREDS OF TIMES OVER FOR WHAT SHE'S PUT YOU THROUGH!
WHAT?... WHAT?... WHAT DID I SAY?
139

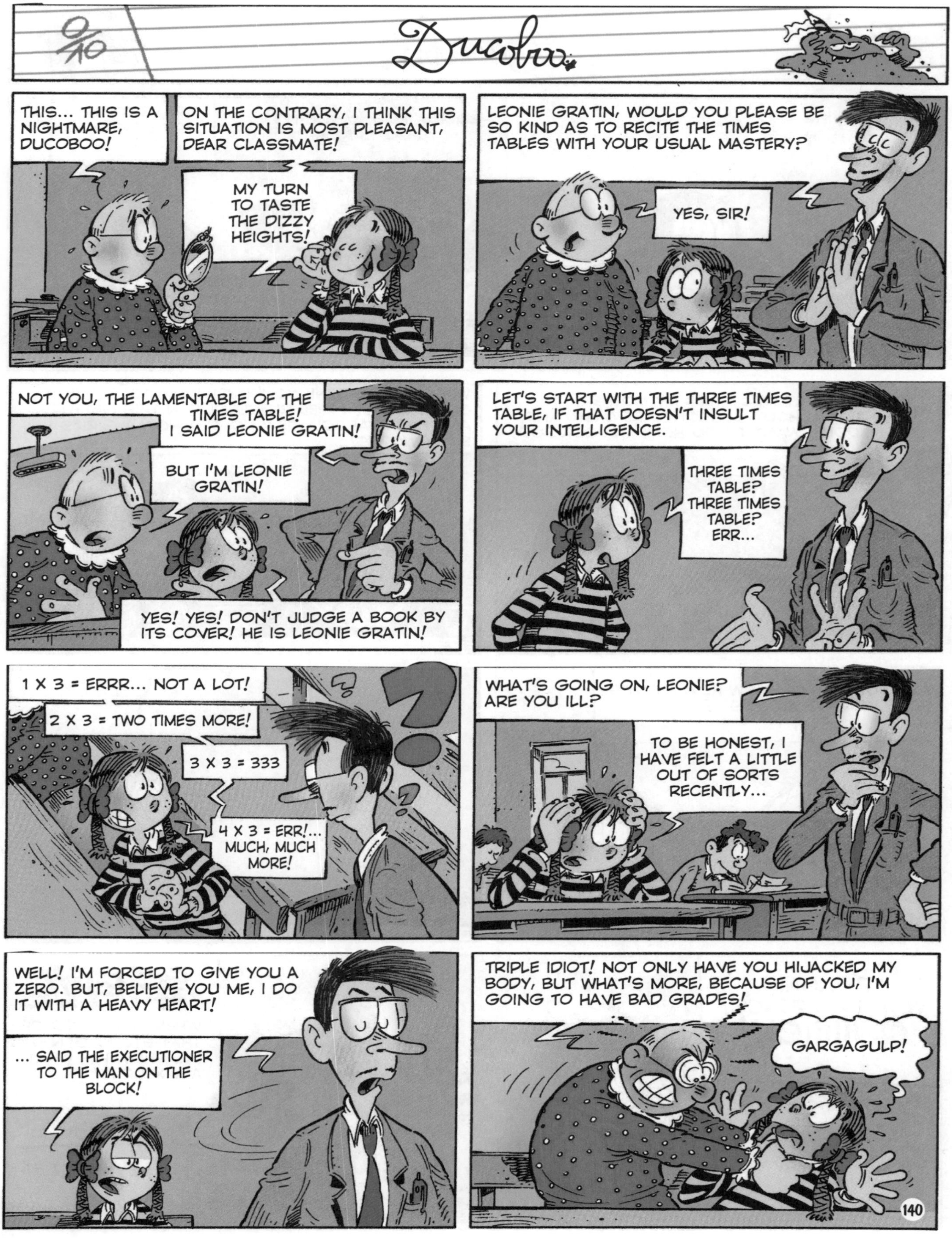
Ducoboo
0/10
THIS... THIS IS A NIGHTMARE, DUCOBOO!
ON THE CONTRARY, I THINK THIS SITUATION IS MOST PLEASANT, DEAR CLASSMATE!
MY TURN TO TASTE THE DIZZY HEIGHTS!
LEONIE GRATIN, WOULD YOU PLEASE BE SO KIND AS TO RECITE THE TIMES TABLES WITH YOUR USUAL MASTERY?
YES, SIR!
NOT YOU, THE LAMENTABLE OF THE TIMES TABLE! I SAID LEONIE GRATIN!
BUT I'M LEONIE GRATIN!
YES! YES! DON'T JUDGE A BOOK BY ITS COVER! HE IS LEONIE GRATIN!
LET'S START WITH THE THREE TIMES TABLE, IF THAT DOESN'T INSULT YOUR INTELLIGENCE.
THREE TIMES TABLE? THREE TIMES TABLE? ERR...
1 X 3 = ERRR... NOT A LOT!
2 X 3 = TWO TIMES MORE!
3 X 3 = 333
4 X 3 = ERR!... MUCH, MUCH MORE!
WHAT'S GOING ON, LEONIE? ARE YOU ILL?
TO BE HONEST, I HAVE FELT A LITTLE OUT OF SORTS RECENTLY...
WELL! I'M FORCED TO GIVE YOU A ZERO. BUT, BELIEVE YOU ME, I DO IT WITH A HEAVY HEART!
... SAID THE EXECUTIONER TO THE MAN ON THE BLOCK!
TRIPLE IDIOT! NOT ONLY HAVE YOU HIJACKED MY BODY, BUT WHAT'S MORE, BECAUSE OF YOU, I'M GOING TO HAVE BAD GRADES!
GARGAGULP!
140

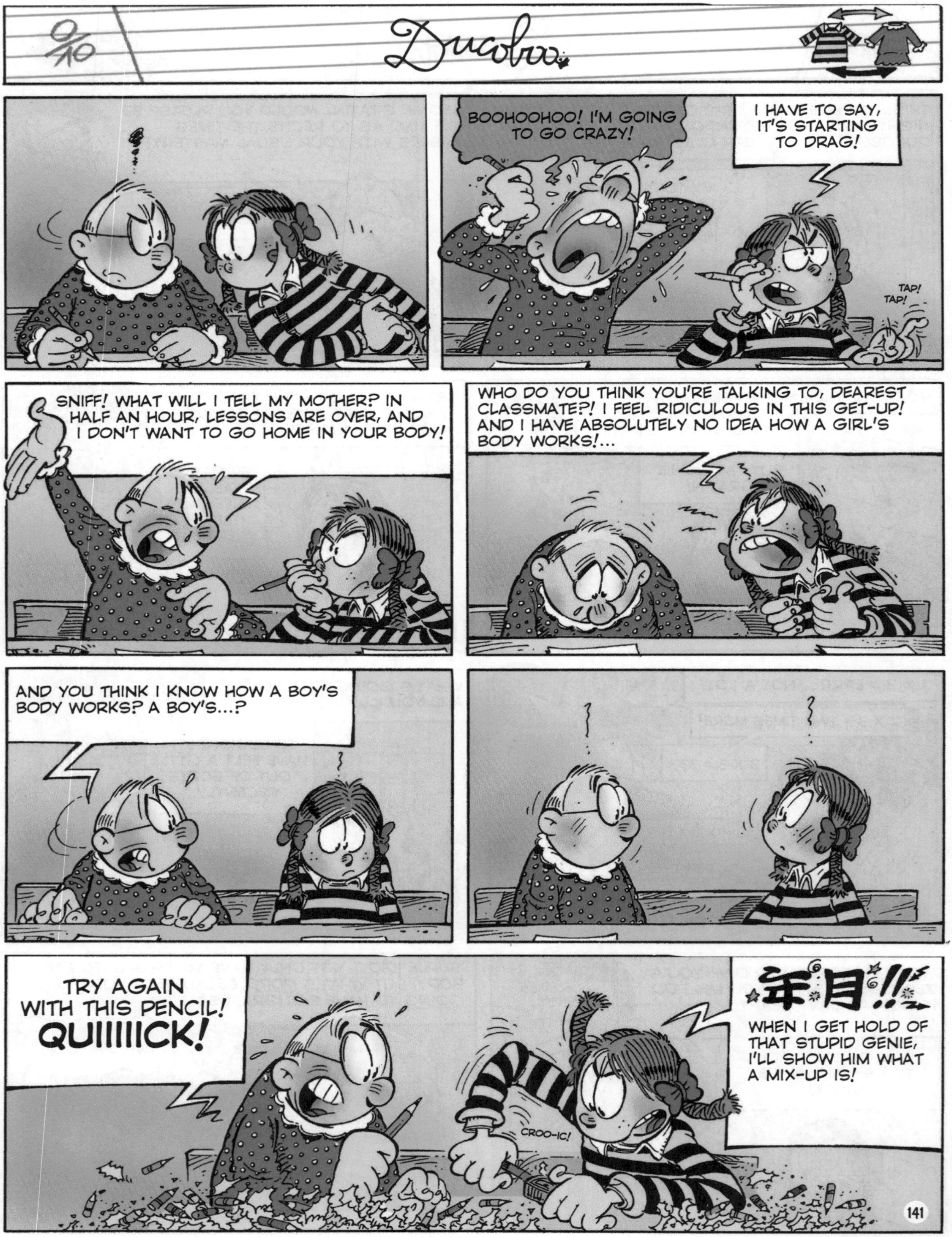
Ducobu
BOOHOOHOO! I'M GOING TO GO CRAZY!
I HAVE TO SAY, IT'S STARTING TO DRAG!
TAP! TAP!
SNIFF! WHAT WILL I TELL MY MOTHER? IN HALF AN HOUR, LESSONS ARE OVER, AND I DON'T WANT TO GO HOME IN YOUR BODY!
WHO DO YOU THINK YOU'RE TALKING TO, DEAREST CLASSMATE?! I FEEL RIDICULOUS IN THIS GET-UP! AND I HAVE ABSOLUTELY NO IDEA HOW A GIRL'S BODY WORKS!...
AND YOU THINK I KNOW HOW A BOY'S BODY WORKS? A BOY'S...?
TRY AGAIN WITH THIS PENCIL! QUIIIIICK!
WHEN I GET HOLD OF THAT STUPID GENIE, I'LL SHOW HIM WHAT A MIX-UP IS!
CROO-IC!
141

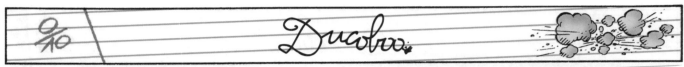

MAY YOUR WISH BE MY COMMAND, MASTER!

COWABUNGA!

ZWUF!

AAAH! IT'S GOOD TO BE BACK IN MY BODY!

MY FAT ROLLS! MY PRECIOUS LITTLE FAT ROLLS! SNIFF!

NOW, DUCOBOO, GIVE ME THE CURSED SHARPENER AND ITS JOKER GENIE SO I CAN STOP THEM FROM DOING ANY MORE HARM, EVER!

NO! I'M STILL ALLOWED ONE MORE WISH AND I WANT IT!

SPEAK, MASTER, AND I WILL OBEY!

DUCOBOO! NO!

SO, HERE'S MY LAST WISH...

WHAT DID YOU ASK HIM FOR?

TO DO MY LINES FOR ME!

AND I DON'T WANT TO SEE THE SLIGHTEST MISTAKE, GOT IT?!

YES, MASTER! GOOD, MASTER!

142

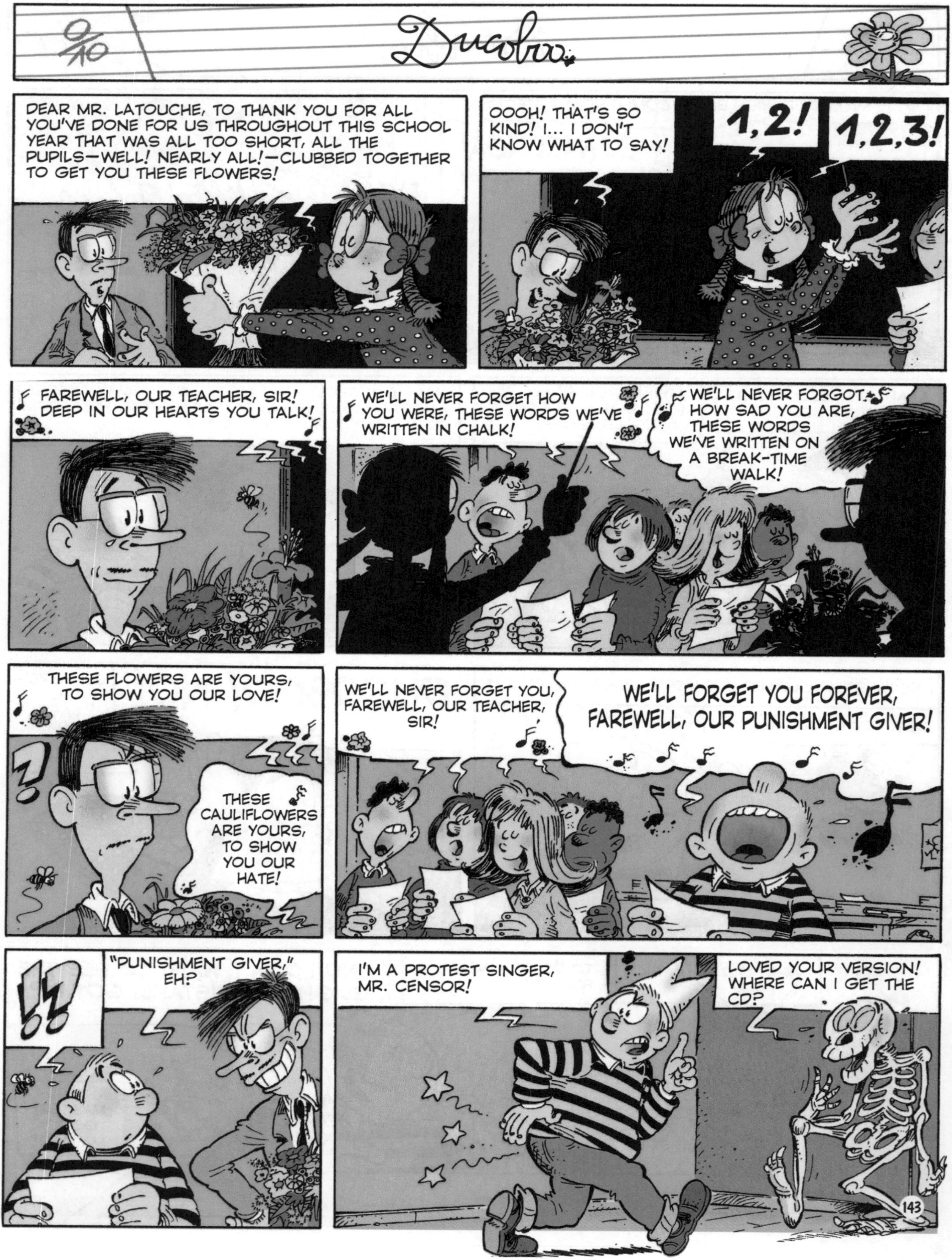
9/10
Ducobu
DEAR MR. LATOUCHE, TO THANK YOU FOR ALL YOU'VE DONE FOR US THROUGHOUT THIS SCHOOL YEAR THAT WAS ALL TOO SHORT, ALL THE PUPILS—WELL! NEARLY ALL!—CLUBBED TOGETHER TO GET YOU THESE FLOWERS!
OOOH! THAT'S SO KIND! I... I DON'T KNOW WHAT TO SAY!
1,2!
1,2,3!
FAREWELL, OUR TEACHER, SIR! DEEP IN OUR HEARTS YOU TALK!
WE'LL NEVER FORGET HOW YOU WERE, THESE WORDS WE'VE WRITTEN IN CHALK!
WE'LL NEVER FORGOT HOW SAD YOU ARE, THESE WORDS WE'VE WRITTEN ON A BREAK-TIME WALK!
THESE FLOWERS ARE YOURS, TO SHOW YOU OUR LOVE!
THESE CAULIFLOWERS ARE YOURS, TO SHOW YOU OUR HATE!
WE'LL NEVER FORGET YOU, FAREWELL, OUR TEACHER, SIR!
WE'LL FORGET YOU FOREVER, FAREWELL, OUR PUNISHMENT GIVER!
"PUNISHMENT GIVER," EH?
I'M A PROTEST SINGER, MR. CENSOR!
LOVED YOUR VERSION! WHERE CAN I GET THE CD?
143

AND SO IT WAS! THE SCHOOL YEAR ALREADY OVER, AS USUAL. JUNE BROUGHT THE YEAR'S HARVEST WITH A 10 OUT OF 10. FOR THE TOP-OF-THE-CLASS PUPILS, TWO LONG MONTHS OF HOLIDAY BEGAN.

A TICKET FOR BREEZE-ON-SEA, PLEASE!

THE SAME, PLEASE!

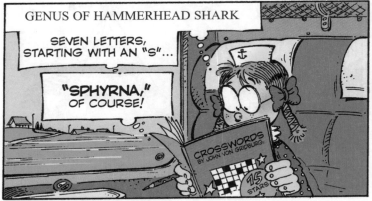

GENUS OF HAMMERHEAD SHARK

SEVEN LETTERS, STARTING WITH AN "S"...

"SPHYRNA," OF COURSE!

CROSSWORDS BY JOHN VON GRIDBURG

15 STARS

THESE CROSSWORDS ARE PATHETICALLY EASY!

S P H Y R N A

MONKEYS' FAVOURITE FRUIT

SIX LETTERS STARTING WITH A "B"...

"BANARNAS", OF COURSE!

MY FIRST CROSSWORDS

?

A R N A

OH, NO! THAT'S RIGHT; THERE'S 7 LETTERS IN "BANARNAS"!

145a

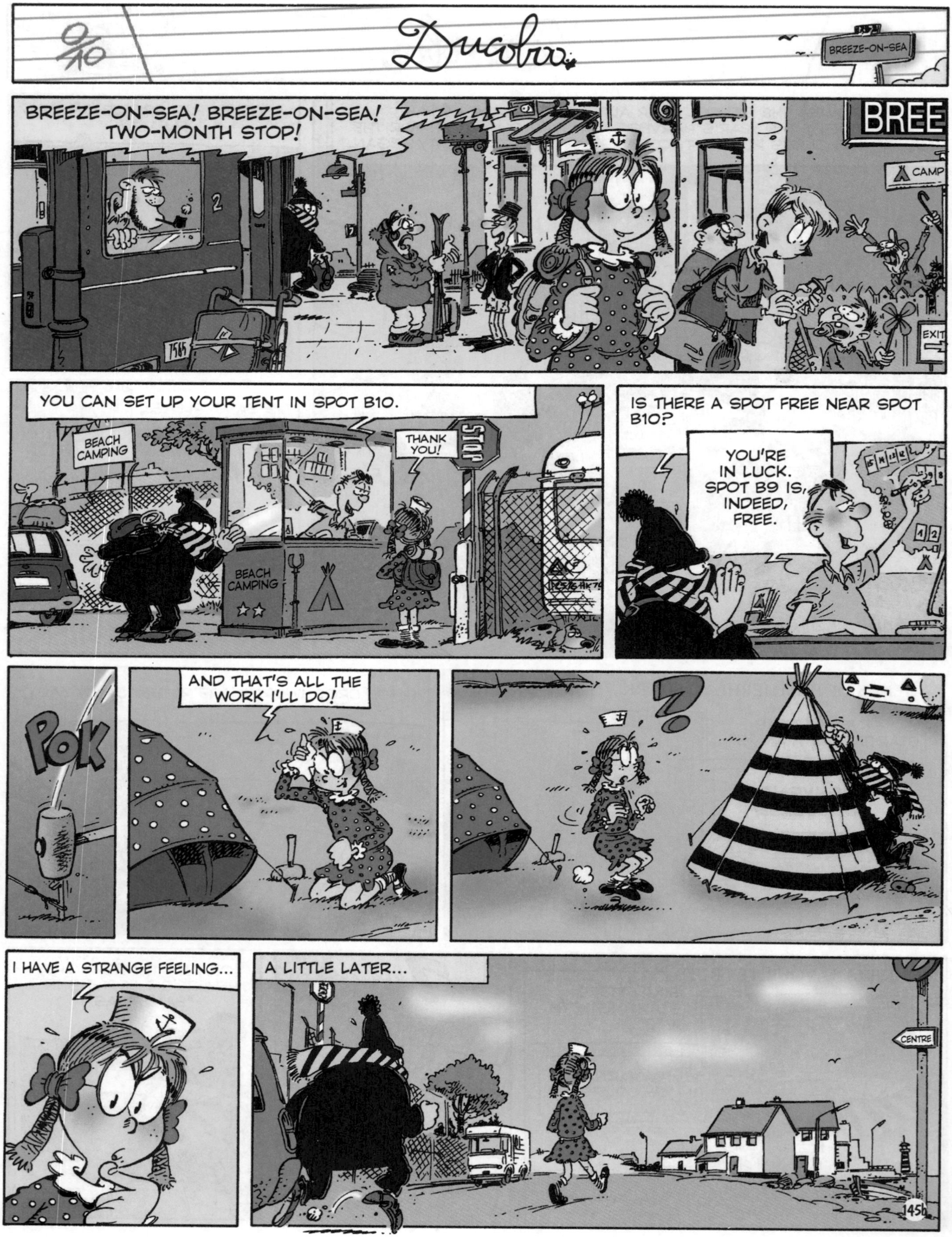

Ducobu
BREEZE-ON-SEA
BREEZE-ON-SEA! BREEZE-ON-SEA! TWO-MONTH STOP!
BREE
CAMP
EXIT
YOU CAN SET UP YOUR TENT IN SPOT B10.
BEACH CAMPING
THANK YOU!
STOP
BEACH CAMPING
IS THERE A SPOT FREE NEAR SPOT B10?
YOU'RE IN LUCK. SPOT B9 IS, INDEED, FREE.
POK
AND THAT'S ALL THE WORK I'LL DO!
I HAVE A STRANGE FEELING...
A LITTLE LATER...
CENTRE
145b

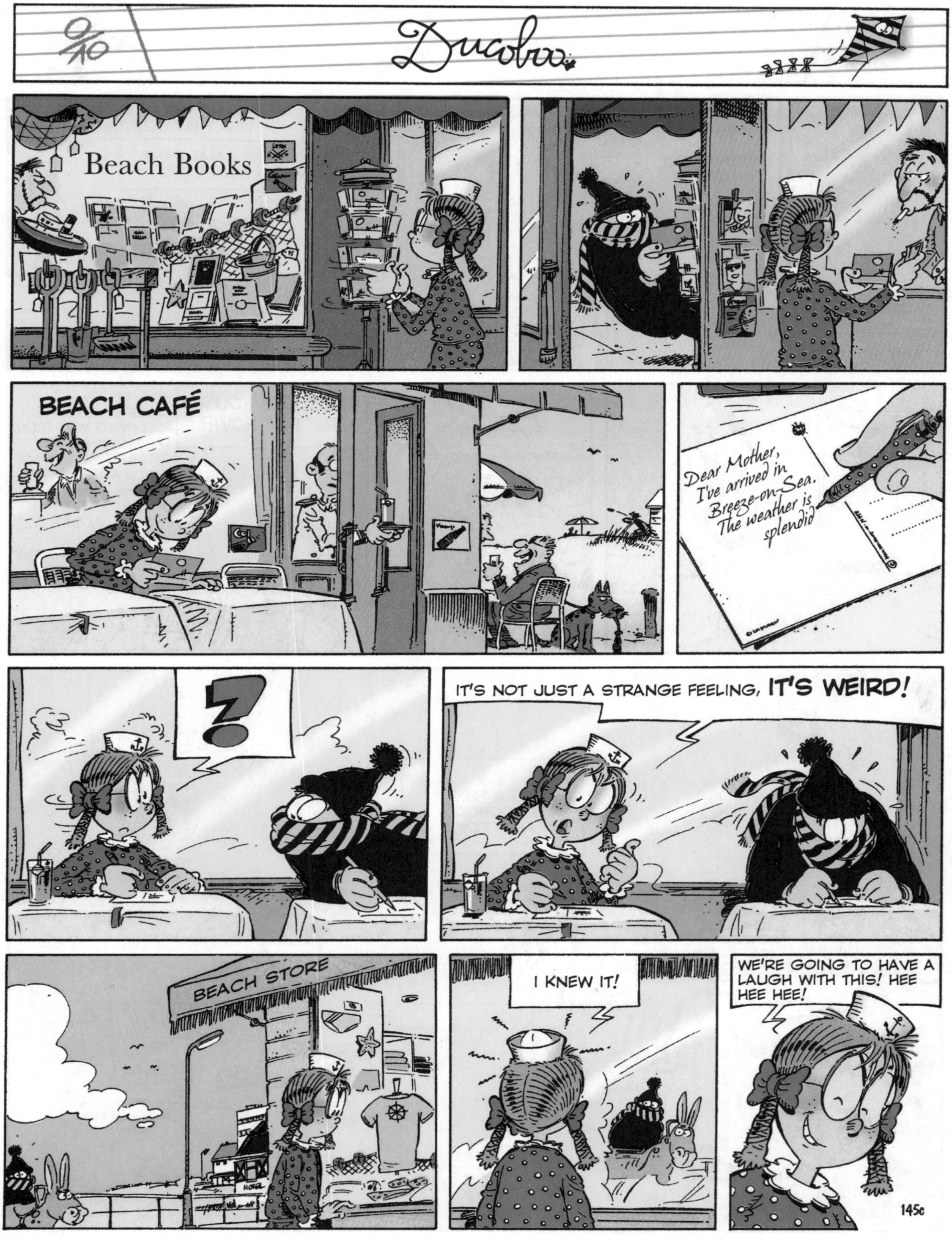

9/10
Ducobu
Beach Books
BEACH CAFÉ
Dear Mother,
I've arrived in
Breeze-on-Sea.
The weather is
splendid
?
IT'S NOT JUST A STRANGE FEELING, IT'S WEIRD!
BEACH STORE
I KNEW IT!
WE'RE GOING TO HAVE A LAUGH WITH THIS! HEE HEE HEE!
145c

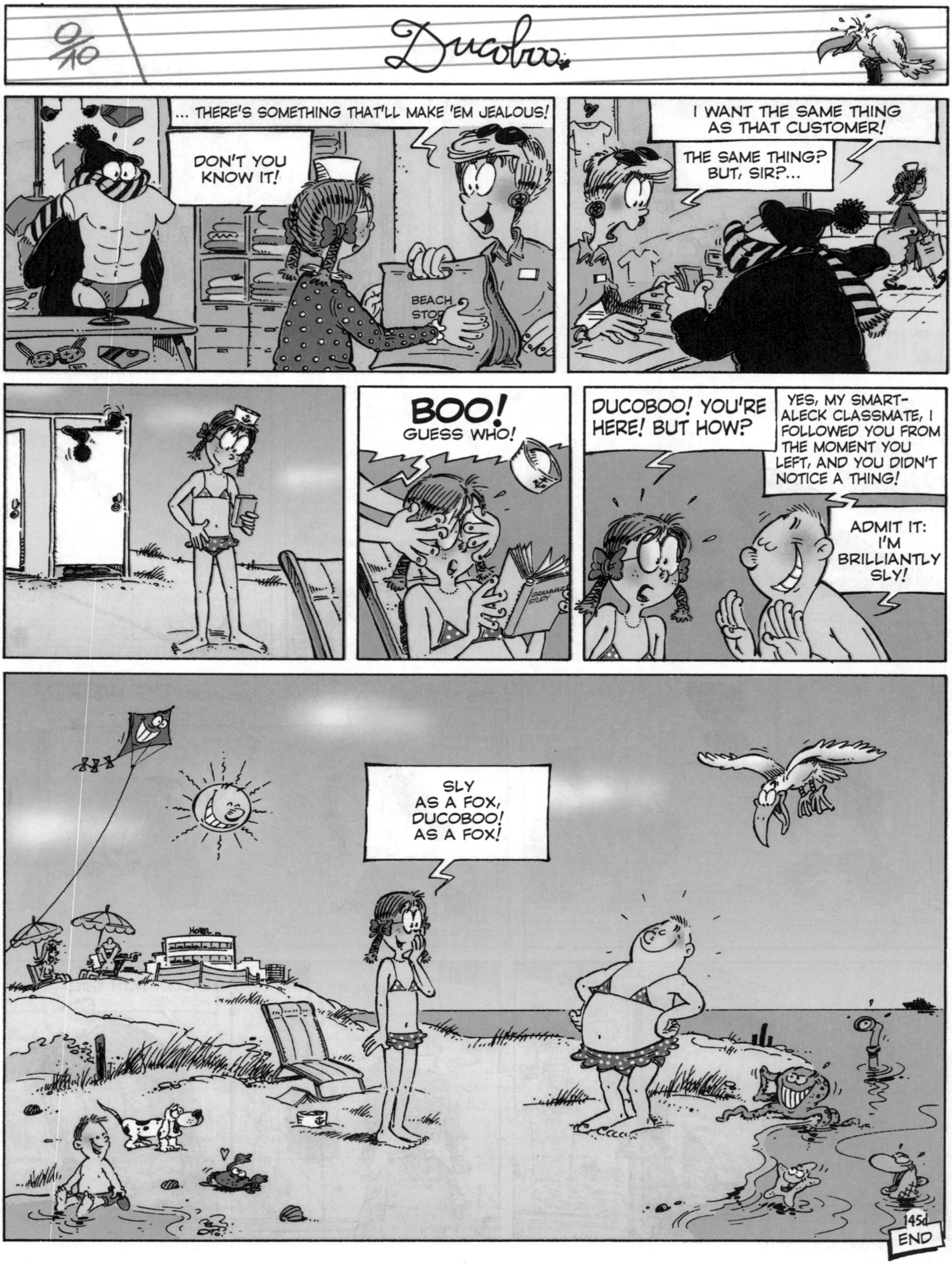
0/10
Ducoboo
... THERE'S SOMETHING THAT'LL MAKE 'EM JEALOUS!
DON'T YOU KNOW IT!
BEACH STO
I WANT THE SAME THING AS THAT CUSTOMER!
THE SAME THING? BUT, SIR?...
BOO! GUESS WHO!
GRAMMAR STUDY
DUCOBOO! YOU'RE HERE! BUT HOW?
YES, MY SMART-ALECK CLASSMATE, I FOLLOWED YOU FROM THE MOMENT YOU LEFT, AND YOU DIDN'T NOTICE A THING!
ADMIT IT: I'M BRILLIANTLY SLY!
SLY AS A FOX, DUCOBOO! AS A FOX!
HOTEL
145d
END

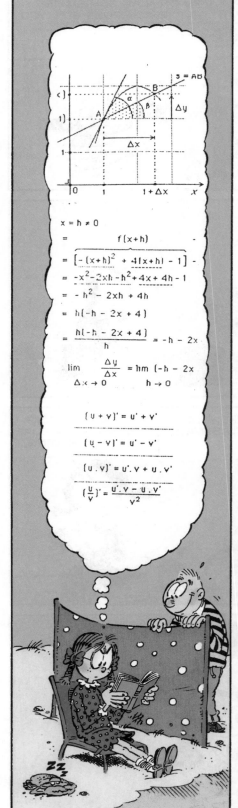

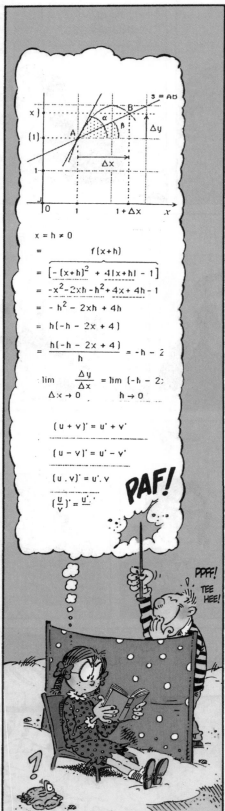

PAF!

PPFF! TEE HEE!

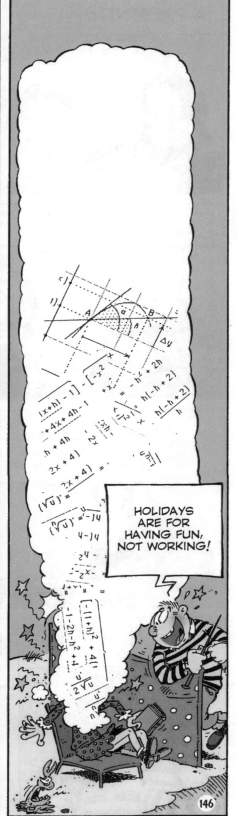

HOLIDAYS ARE FOR HAVING FUN, NOT WORKING!

146

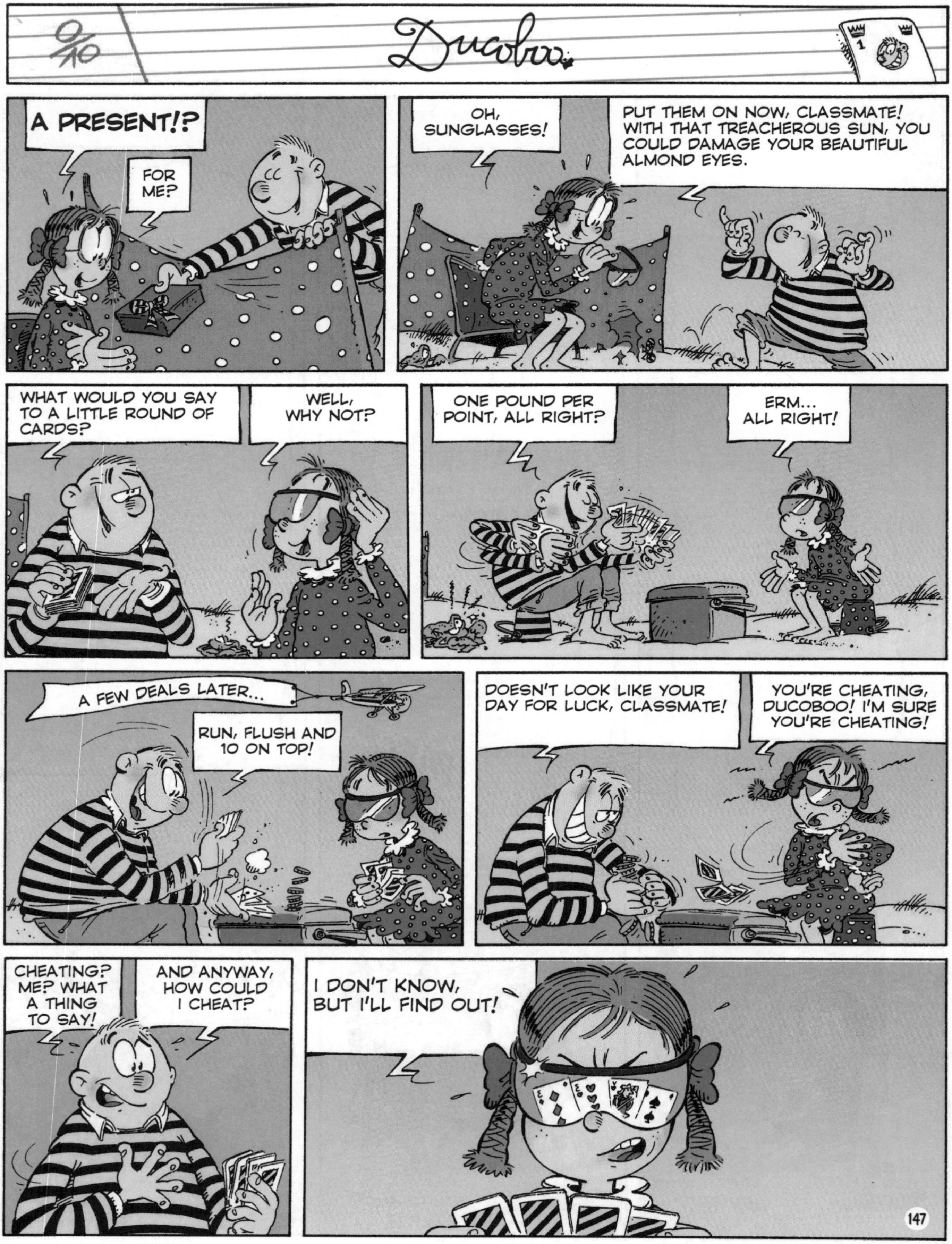
Ducoboo
A PRESENT!?
FOR ME?
OH, SUNGLASSES!
PUT THEM ON NOW, CLASSMATE! WITH THAT TREACHEROUS SUN, YOU COULD DAMAGE YOUR BEAUTIFUL ALMOND EYES.
WHAT WOULD YOU SAY TO A LITTLE ROUND OF CARDS?
WELL, WHY NOT?
ONE POUND PER POINT, ALL RIGHT?
ERM... ALL RIGHT!
A FEW DEALS LATER...
RUN, FLUSH AND 10 ON TOP!
DOESN'T LOOK LIKE YOUR DAY FOR LUCK, CLASSMATE!
YOU'RE CHEATING, DUCOBOO! I'M SURE YOU'RE CHEATING!
CHEATING? ME? WHAT A THING TO SAY!
AND ANYWAY, HOW COULD I CHEAT?
I DON'T KNOW, BUT I'LL FIND OUT!
147

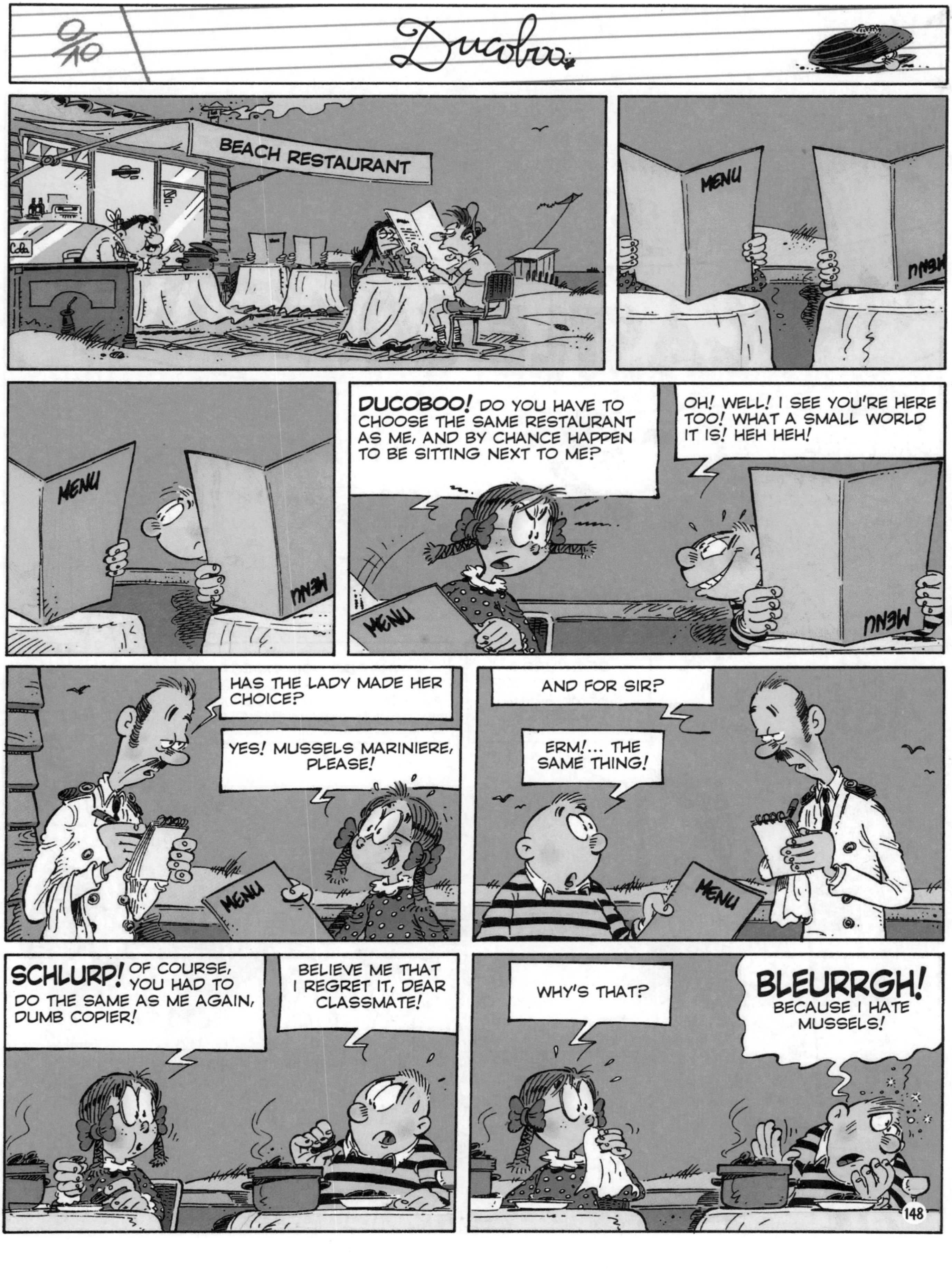
9/10
Ducoboo
BEACH RESTAURANT
Cola
MENU
MENU
MENU
MENU
MENU
DUCOBOO! DO YOU HAVE TO CHOOSE THE SAME RESTAURANT AS ME, AND BY CHANCE HAPPEN TO BE SITTING NEXT TO ME?
OH! WELL! I SEE YOU'RE HERE TOO! WHAT A SMALL WORLD IT IS! HEH HEH!
MENU
MENU
HAS THE LADY MADE HER CHOICE?
YES! MUSSELS MARINIERE, PLEASE!
MENU
AND FOR SIR?
ERM!... THE SAME THING!
MENU
SCHLURP! OF COURSE, YOU HAD TO DO THE SAME AS ME AGAIN, DUMB COPIER!
BELIEVE ME THAT I REGRET IT, DEAR CLASSMATE!
WHY'S THAT?
BLEURRGH! BECAUSE I HATE MUSSELS!
148

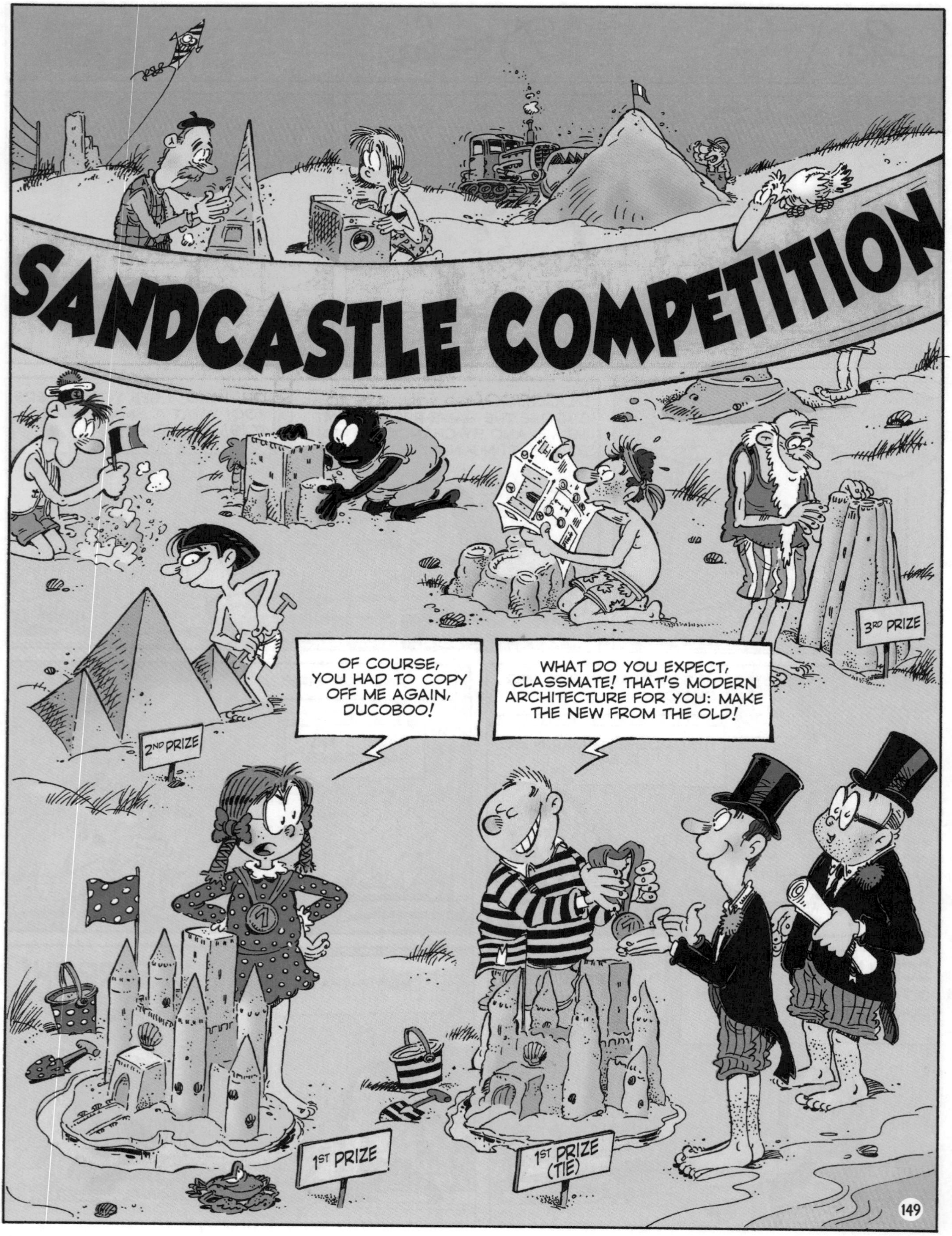
SANDCASTLE COMPETITION
3RD PRIZE
2ND PRIZE
OF COURSE, YOU HAD TO COPY OFF ME AGAIN, DUCOBOO!
WHAT DO YOU EXPECT, CLASSMATE! THAT'S MODERN ARCHITECTURE FOR YOU: MAKE THE NEW FROM THE OLD!
1ST PRIZE
1ST PRIZE (TIE)
149

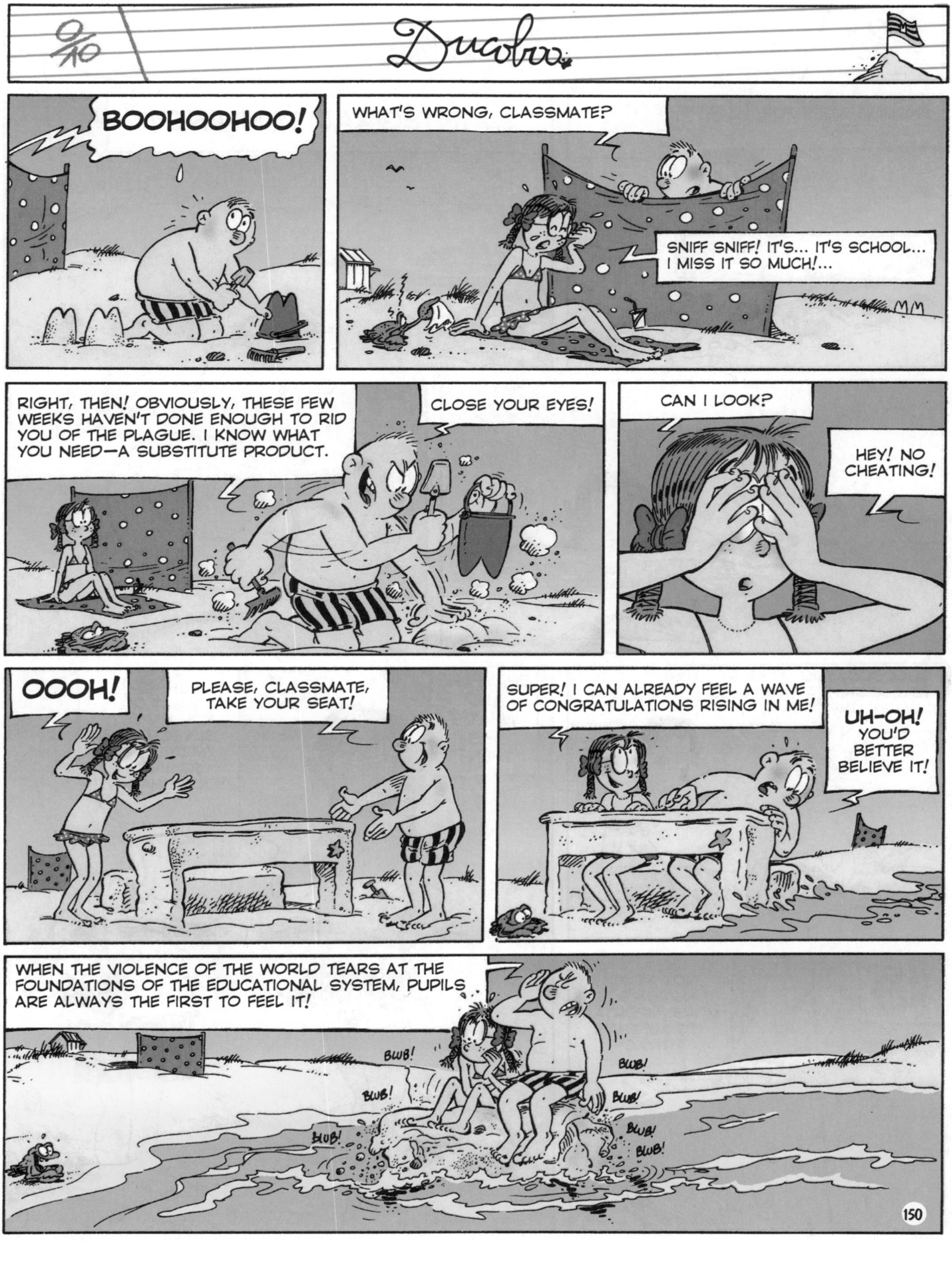
0/10
Ducobu
BOOHOOHOO!
WHAT'S WRONG, CLASSMATE?
SNIFF SNIFF! IT'S... IT'S SCHOOL... I MISS IT SO MUCH!...
RIGHT, THEN! OBVIOUSLY, THESE FEW WEEKS HAVEN'T DONE ENOUGH TO RID YOU OF THE PLAGUE. I KNOW WHAT YOU NEED—A SUBSTITUTE PRODUCT.
CLOSE YOUR EYES!
CAN I LOOK?
HEY! NO CHEATING!
OOOH!
PLEASE, CLASSMATE, TAKE YOUR SEAT!
SUPER! I CAN ALREADY FEEL A WAVE OF CONGRATULATIONS RISING IN ME!
UH-OH! YOU'D BETTER BELIEVE IT!
WHEN THE VIOLENCE OF THE WORLD TEARS AT THE FOUNDATIONS OF THE EDUCATIONAL SYSTEM, PUPILS ARE ALWAYS THE FIRST TO FEEL IT!
BLUB!
BLUB!
BLUB!
BLUB!
BLUB!
BLUB!
BLUB!
150

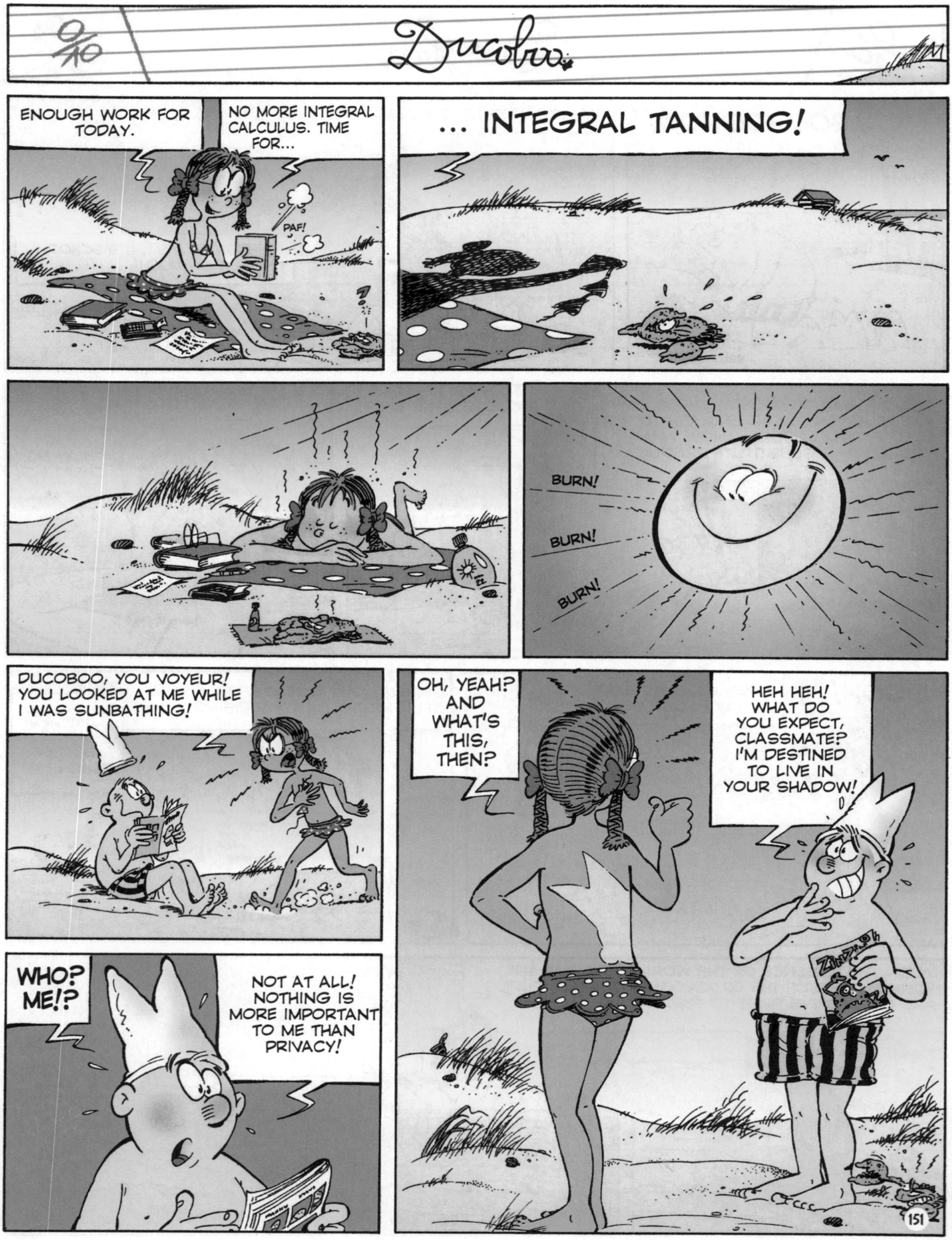
Ducoboo
ENOUGH WORK FOR TODAY.
NO MORE INTEGRAL CALCULUS. TIME FOR...
PAF!
... INTEGRAL TANNING!
BURN!
BURN!
BURN!
DUCOBOO, YOU VOYEUR! YOU LOOKED AT ME WHILE I WAS SUNBATHING!
WHO? ME!?
NOT AT ALL! NOTHING IS MORE IMPORTANT TO ME THAN PRIVACY!
OH, YEAH? AND WHAT'S THIS, THEN?
HEH HEH! WHAT DO YOU EXPECT, CLASSMATE? I'M DESTINED TO LIVE IN YOUR SHADOW!
151

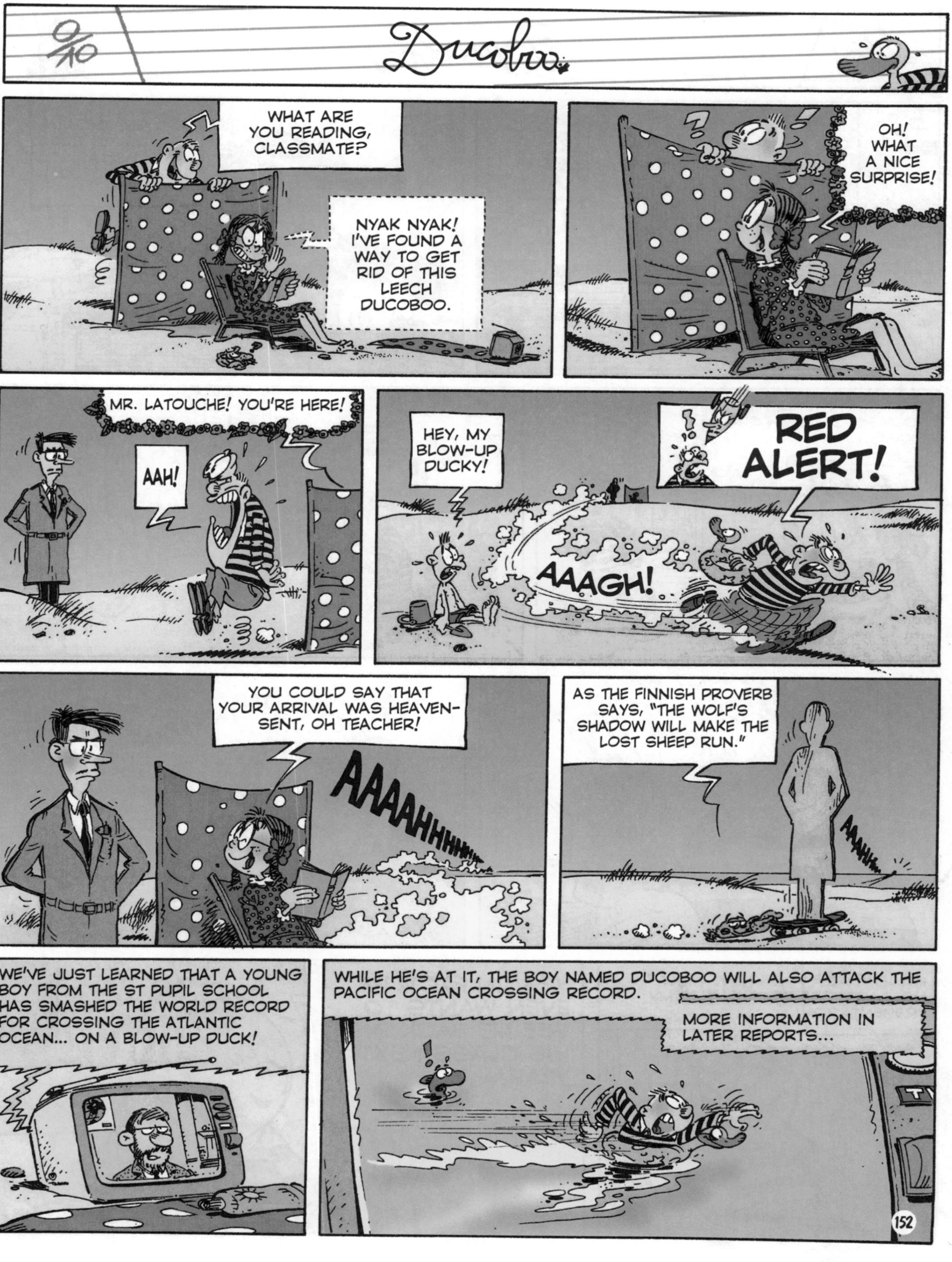
Ducoboo
WHAT ARE YOU READING, CLASSMATE?
NYAK NYAK! I'VE FOUND A WAY TO GET RID OF THIS LEECH DUCOBOO.
OH! WHAT A NICE SURPRISE!
MR. LATOUCHE! YOU'RE HERE!
AAH!
HEY, MY BLOW-UP DUCKY!
RED ALERT!
AAAGH!
YOU COULD SAY THAT YOUR ARRIVAL WAS HEAVEN-SENT, OH TEACHER!
AAAAAHHHH
AS THE FINNISH PROVERB SAYS, "THE WOLF'S SHADOW WILL MAKE THE LOST SHEEP RUN."
WE'VE JUST LEARNED THAT A YOUNG BOY FROM THE ST PUPIL SCHOOL HAS SMASHED THE WORLD RECORD FOR CROSSING THE ATLANTIC OCEAN... ON A BLOW-UP DUCK!
WHILE HE'S AT IT, THE BOY NAMED DUCOBOO WILL ALSO ATTACK THE PACIFIC OCEAN CROSSING RECORD.
MORE INFORMATION IN LATER REPORTS...
152

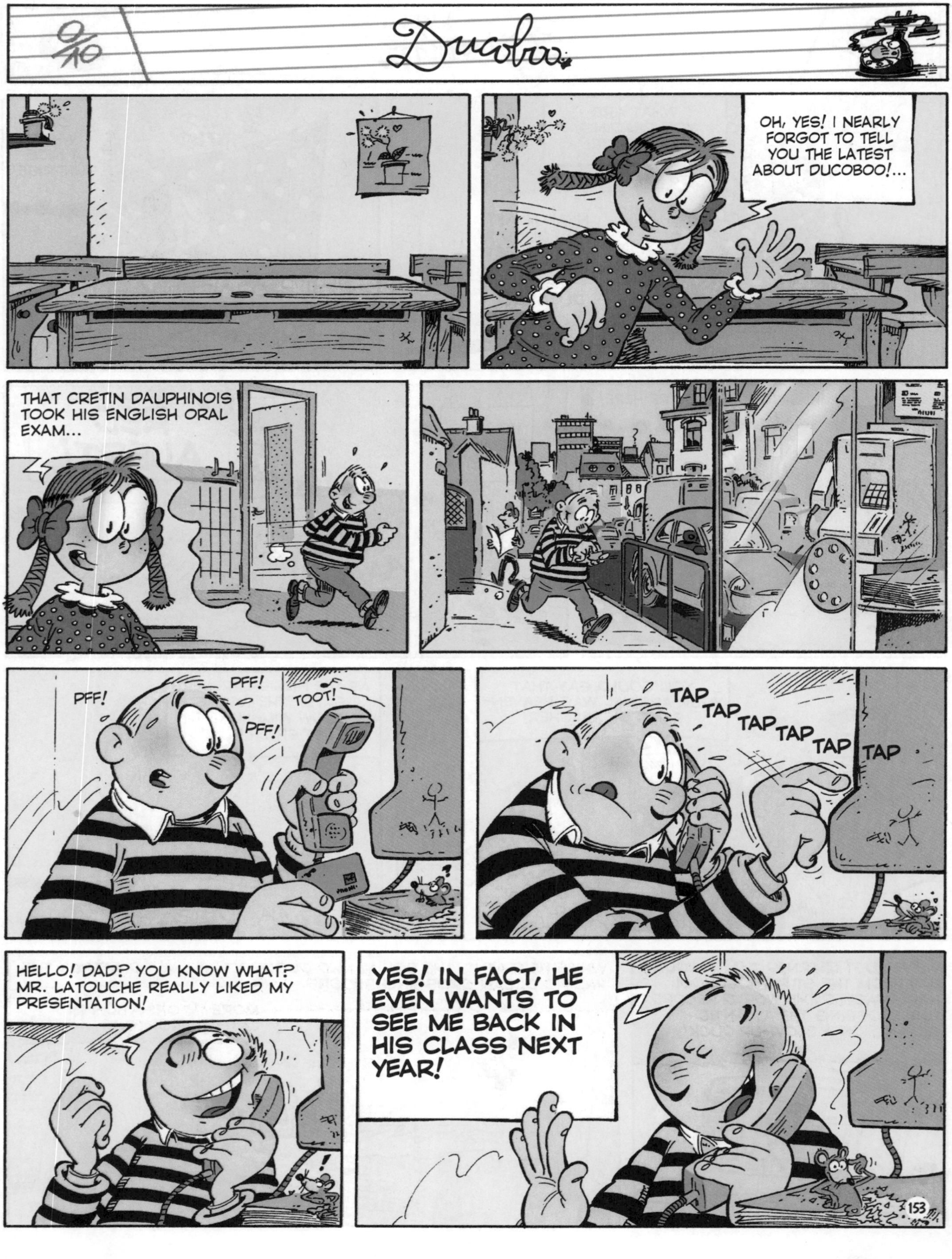
0/10
Ducoboo
OH, YES! I NEARLY FORGOT TO TELL YOU THE LATEST ABOUT DUCOBOO!...
THAT CRETIN DAUPHINOIS TOOK HIS ENGLISH ORAL EXAM...
PFF!
PFF!
PFF!
TOOT!
TAP TAP TAP TAP TAP TAP
HELLO! DAD? YOU KNOW WHAT? MR. LATOUCHE REALLY LIKED MY PRESENTATION!
YES! IN FACT, HE EVEN WANTS TO SEE ME BACK IN HIS CLASS NEXT YEAR!
153

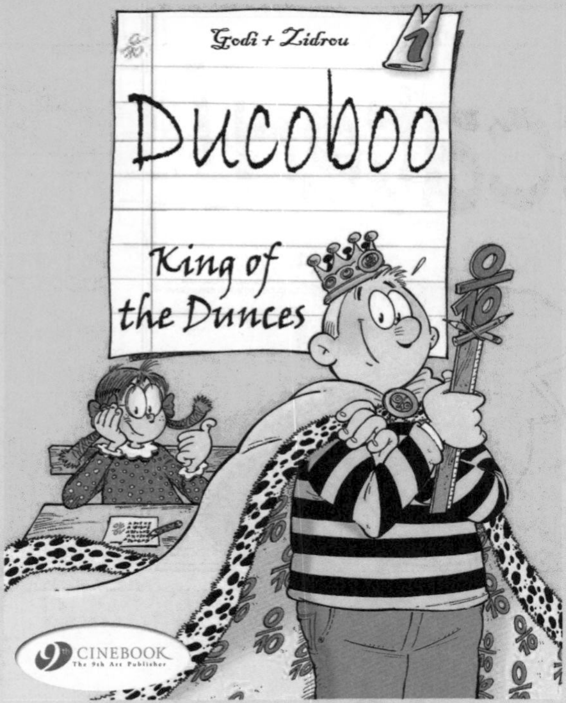
Godi + Zidrou
1
Ducoboo
King of the Dunces
CINEBOOK
The 9th Art Publisher

1 - King of the Dunces

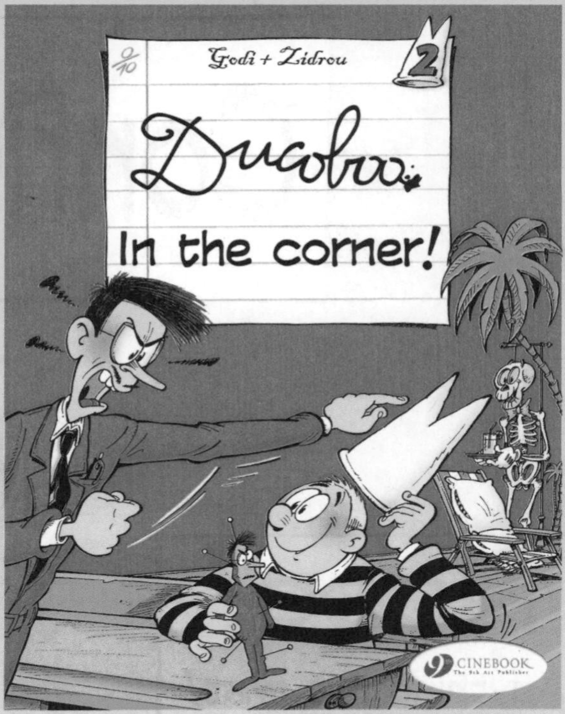
Godi + Zidrou
2
Ducoboo
In the corner!
CINEBOOK
The 9th Art Publisher

2 - In the Corner!

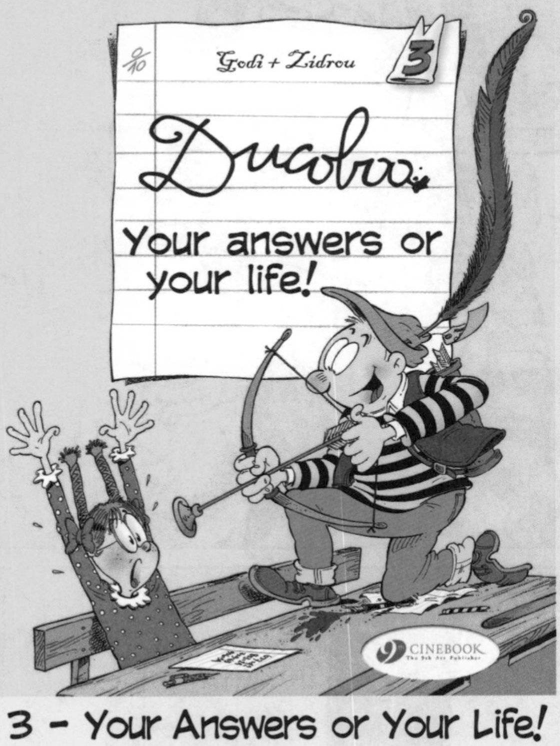
Godi + Zidrou
3
Ducoboo
Your answers or your life!
CINEBOOK
The 9th Art Publisher

3 - Your Answers or Your Life!

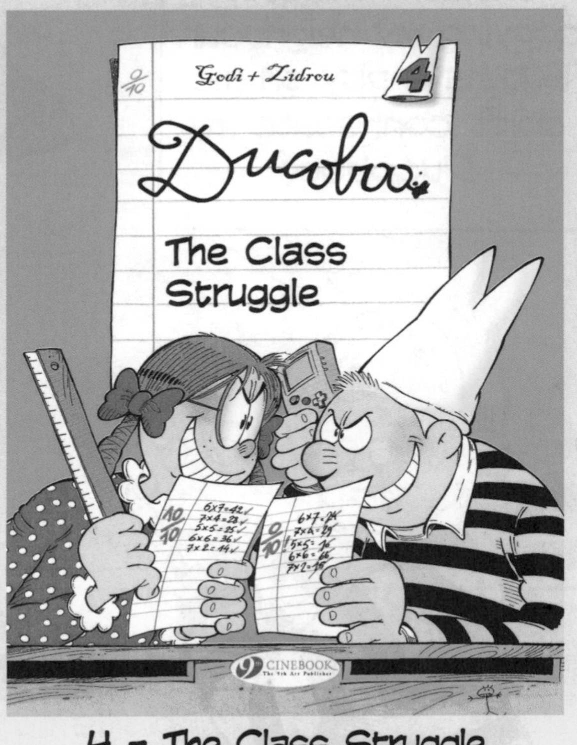
Godi + Zidrou
4
Ducoboo
The Class Struggle
CINEBOOK
The 9th Art Publisher

4 - The Class Struggle

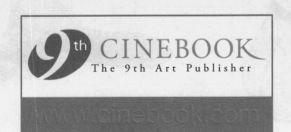

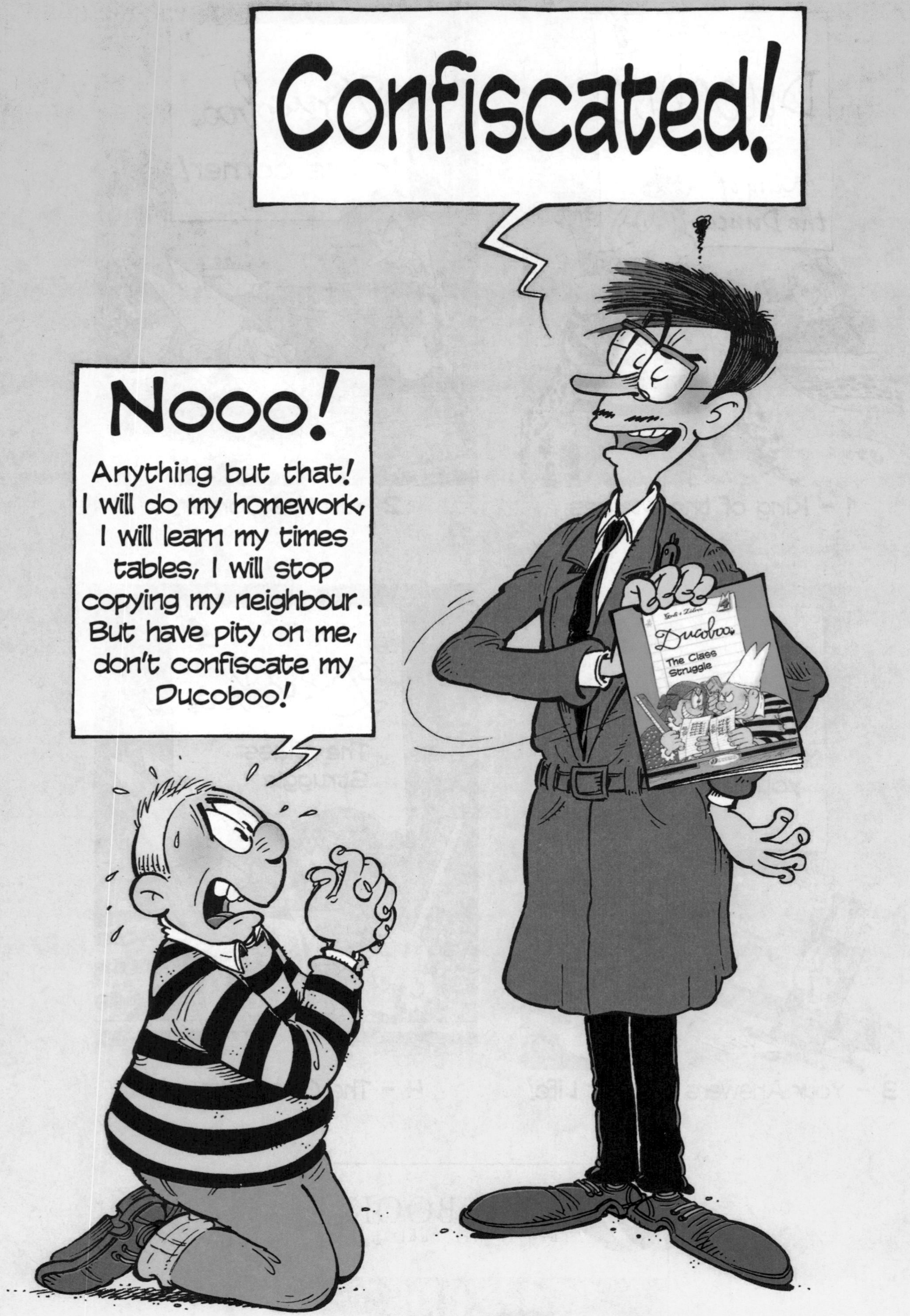
Confiscated!
Nooo! Anything but that! I will do my homework, I will learn my times tables, I will stop copying my neighbour. But have pity on me, don't confiscate my Ducoboo!
Ducoboo
The Class Struggle